781 544 343 a

Witches Among Us

The Story of the Salem Witchcraft Trials

by Steven L. Stern

AMSCO

AMSCO SCHOOL PUBLICATIONS, INC.
315 Hudson Street/ New York, NY 10013

To Lisa and Michael, with love.

Text Design by Merrill Haber

Cover Design by A Good Thing, Inc.

Compositor and Artwork: A Good Thing, Inc.

Please visit our Web site at:
www.amscopub.com

When ordering this book, please specify:
either **R 696 P** *or*
WITCHES AMONG US: THE STORY
OF THE SALEM WITCHCRAFT TRIALS

Amsco Originals

ISBN 1-56765-067-8
NYC Item 56765-067-7

Printed in the United States of America

1 2 3 4 5 6 7 8 9 10   04 03 02 01 00

To the Reader

This is a true story. The strange and shocking events described really happened about three hundred years ago. They took place in the Massachusetts Bay Colony in a small farming community called Salem Village.

In 1692, Salem Village was legally part of Salem Town, a busy port five miles to the east. To find Salem Village on a Massachusetts map today, look for the town of Danvers. That's the name Salem Village took when it became independent in 1752.

The records of all that went on before and during the witchcraft trials are not complete. To this day, historians are still trying to piece together all the events and figure out how and why they happened.

Many authors have written about the Salem witchcraft trials. You can find their books and articles in the library. You can even find Web sites on the Internet about the Salem witch hunt. Even today, authors continue to write new books about what happened in Salem Village so many years ago.

All these authors and historians do not always agree. This is not surprising. Many records have been lost. Some facts are just not known. Others are hard to verify. Newer books and older books sometimes interpret events differently. Sometimes they disagree about details. However, most accounts do agree about what basically happened.

In writing *Witches Among Us: The Story of the Salem Witchcraft Trials,* I have tried to keep to the facts. The people, places, and events described are real. At times, though, I have filled in words or details that the historical records do not provide. I've made these additions to help the story flow and to give you, the reader, a better feel for events.

Steven L. Stern

Chapter 1

January, 1692

"Maybe we shouldn't," Betty said. She was getting scared.

"You're forever worrying," Abigail said. She was eleven, two years older than her cousin Betty. Betty always acted like such a baby, Abigail thought.

"But if it's a sin—" Betty started.

"Stop, now," Abigail cut her off. She had heard enough talk from Betty about sin. Betty was sounding more like her father every day.

Betty's father was Reverend Samuel Parris, the minister of Salem Village Church. Abigail Williams lived in the Parris home with Betty and her family. She heard Reverend Parris talk about sin every day—about sin, good and evil, and heaven and hell. In fact, it often seemed like sin and punishment were the only things Reverend Parris talked to them about.

The two girls were sitting at a table in the Parris kitchen. A candle burned against the afternoon dimness. The dark glass of the small windows let in little light. Tituba stood across the room. She was a Caribbean Indian. Tituba and her husband John were slaves who lived with the Parris family. Betty and Abigail spent many hours in Tituba's care.

Tituba often told the girls stories. Sometimes she described what it had been like to live in the West Indies. Sometimes she talked about magic and fortune-telling.

Tituba's stories were so interesting that Betty and Abigail's friends would often come by. Ann Putnam, Mary Walcott, Elizabeth Hubbard, and some of the other girls of the village enjoyed listening, too. These girls were older than Betty and Abigail, most of them in their teens.

Hearing Tituba's tales was a rare treat. Day-to-day life in Salem Village was as serious as it was dull. The people were Puritans. Their lives were devoted to religion and hard work. Activities meant just for amusement were seen as sinful temptations. Any free time was best spent reading the Bible. There was little "fun," even for children. In fact, by age six or seven, children were assigned their fair share of household chores.

Each day was much the same as another. Only Sundays were different. Instead of working, the people attended church for five hours.

The rest of the day they were expected to continue their prayers and religious reading at home. To do otherwise would be to commit a sin.

For Betty, Abigail, and their friends, Tituba's stories added a bright ray of light to the cold and gloomy winter months. Even better, sometimes the girls did more than just talk about fortune-telling. They tried it.

Tituba would study the lines in their palms. She'd predict where a girl would travel or what kind of man she would marry. Sometimes Tituba told the girls what their dreams might mean.

Although the games offered a welcome relief from hours of sewing, spinning, cleaning, washing, and cooking, Betty and some of the others grew uneasy. Did telling fortunes really call upon evil powers, as the ministers warned? Was their behavior sinful? They wondered. They hoped and prayed that it wasn't. Sinners burned in hell. Even children. That was the message they heard hour after hour at church every Sunday.

One day they tried a new fortune-telling game. Someone dropped the white of an egg into a glass of water. All the girls stared at the shapes that slowly formed. They asked questions about their future husbands. They eagerly watched the changing shapes for clues to the answers.

The "egg and glass" soon became a regular part of their meetings. Several of the girls, though, became fearful. They knew they would be in terrible trouble if anyone found out. One girl even whispered that the egg and glass was "a tool of the Devil." At this, Betty almost started to cry. The Devil was very real to the Puritans and very scary. Abigail told her cousin to hush.

Despite Betty's fears, she and Abigail used the egg and glass again—Abigail had insisted. Like all the other girls, she knew that fortune-telling was something they shouldn't be doing. But the snowy New England winter was endless, as were the girls' chores. Anyway, no one but Tituba knew they were playing these games, and Tituba wouldn't tell.

Abigail picked up the egg. Betty protested again.

"What if it really is one of the Devil's tools?" Betty said, her voice trembling. Lately, she'd been having bad dreams. Awful dreams. Dreams about the Devil and the fires of hell. Betty wondered if any of the other girls had also been having trouble sleeping. Surely she couldn't be the only one, even if she was the youngest.

Abigail ignored her. She cracked and separated the egg. Then she poured the white into the glass. The room was silent, except for the flames crackling in the fireplace. Tituba was busying herself on the other side of the kitchen.

Abigail and Betty studied the shiny strands of white drifting down through the glass. The candle flame flickered.

Betty suddenly gasped.

"Do you see that?" she whispered. Her eyes were wide.

"What?"

Betty's heart was pounding. "I think it's . . . it's . . ." She covered her mouth with her hand.

"It's *what*?" The growing fear in her cousin's voice was making Abigail afraid, too. "What do you see?"

"A . . . coffin." Betty was on the verge of tears. "I see a coffin."

Abigail stared hard into the glass. After a moment, she began to see the shape too.

Betty was right. It did look like a coffin.

"Abigail . . . what have we done?" Betty was crying now, big tears rolling down her cheeks. "This is evil! This is Devil's work!"

Abigail felt the icy chill of panic. There must indeed be a reason that such games were forbidden.

"This is Devil's work!" Betty said again, rising from the table. "We will surely feel the wrath of God!" She stumbled back from the table. Her face was pale.

Abigail couldn't take her eyes from the glass. Her throat was suddenly too dry for her to speak. Her heart was beating as fast as her cousin's.

Devil's work. The words burned in Abigail's mind like the flames of hell.

Chapter 2

Salem Village was part of the Massachusetts Bay Colony. It was barely a town by today's standards. Only about 550 people lived in the tiny farming village. Rough dirt roads connected the widely scattered houses and farms. In the distance lay wilderness. The village had a one-room meetinghouse, where church services were held, and a parsonage, where the Parris family lived. There was also an inn, several craftsmen's shops, and a small building for the militiamen who stood watch against Indian attack.

In a village so small, unusual events quickly drew people's attention. It was not long before the people of Salem became aware that something odd was going on.

It started soon after Betty and Abigail had seen the shape of the coffin. Night after night, both girls had terrible nightmares. Sometimes one girl or the other would awaken with a scream, then burst into tears.

Reverend and Mrs. Parris were concerned. So was Tituba. Again and again they asked the girls what was the matter. But Betty and Abigail wouldn't say. Sometimes they exchanged silent looks, as though sharing a guilty secret.

Soon the girls' worrisome behavior spread to the daytime. First Betty, then Abigail, began acting strangely. The girls crawled under chairs and into holes. They cried out for no reason. They made peculiar sounds and movements. Sometimes they just sat and stared straight ahead. Other times they ran about flapping their arms like wings. Sometimes they babbled words that no one could understand.

Reverend Parris did not know what to make of any of this. His concerns grew. What illness could cause his daughter and his niece to act this way? He prayed for their recovery, but the girls only got worse.

Reverend Parris sent for one doctor, then another. The doctors shook their heads, puzzled. Their treatments did no good.

Within a few weeks, Betty and Abigail began having fits. One minute the girls would be fine. The next, their bodies would twist into impossible positions. They would be unable to speak. Sometimes they would seem to be choking.

By mid-February, the girls' fits were becoming more and more violent. Reverend Parris was frantic. He sent for Dr. William Griggs, who lived nearby. Dr. Griggs was the great-uncle of Elizabeth Hubbard, one of the girls who had sometimes come to hear Tituba's stories.

Dr. Griggs had examined the girls before. He had checked his medical books. But, like the other doctors, he had been unable to explain the girls' mysterious illness.

Now, as Dr. Griggs stood helplessly before the two young girls, he shook his head. Then he took Reverend Parris aside.

"This is very serious," the doctor said.

"But surely there is something you can do," Reverend Parris insisted. "Some medicine . . . some treatment . . ."

Dr. Griggs met the minister's dark brown eyes. The doctor hesitated. He did not want to say what he was thinking.

"Speak, then," Reverend Parris urged.

When the doctor finally replied, his voice was just above a whisper.

"I fear, Minister, that the girls are under an evil hand."

Reverend Parris stared at him. "You say that . . . they are afflicted by . . . *witchcraft?*"

The doctor nodded grimly. "I have thought long and hard on it, Minister. I can think of no other explanation."

Chapter 3

Word of the girls' bewitchment spread from neighbor to neighbor. The people of Salem Village reacted with both curiosity and concern. Many visited the Parris home, wanting to see "the afflicted girls" for themselves.

Many people in Salem Village did not like or support Reverend Parris. They thought him vain and harsh. During his four years in Salem, the minister had made more than his share of enemies. What would people say now? he wondered. What would talk of witchcraft do to his reputation? To his standing in the community? Would the people demand a new minister?

Reverend Parris invited to his home several ministers and other respected men from nearby towns. He wanted their advice and support. Reverend John Hale of Beverly came. So did Reverend Nicholas Noyes of Salem Town.

The men observed the afflicted girls. They talked matters over. Finally, they agreed with Dr.

Griggs. The hand of the Devil was at work in Salem.

The ministers and other men told Reverend Parris to be patient. They advised him to pray and to look to God for guidance.

Before they left, the men questioned the slave Tituba. Reverend Parris had told them that lately the girls had begun to see strange visions. Tituba appeared in many of these visions. The girls said that Tituba's "shape" pinched them or stuck invisible pins in their flesh.

Tituba looked from one man to the next. She was bewildered by all that was happening. She tried to answer their questions as best she could. "I am not a witch," she told them again and again. "I would not harm Betty and Abigail."

The men kept firing questions at her. Finally, Tituba admitted that, yes, she did know a little about spells. She had learned some things during her years living on the island of Barbados. But she still insisted that she was not a witch.

Reverend Parris was not satisfied. After the other men left, he kept after Tituba. If the slave knew about spells, then surely she was responsible for the girls' condition.

The more Tituba denied, the angrier the minister became. Day after day, he tried to force her to admit to being a witch. Her confession would help him save not just his daughter and niece but also his position as minister.

Meanwhile, the girls' fits continued. Sometimes it seemed that the more attention Betty and Abigail got, the worse their fits became. Instead of being punished for playing forbidden games, as they'd feared, the girls had become the objects of everyone's interest and concern.

Salem Village buzzed with questions. Who was bewitching the girls? Was it the slave Tituba? Or, could it be someone else? The people began eyeing one another with suspicion—and fear.

Chapter 4

Belief in witches, like belief in the Devil, was gravely serious to 17th-century New Englanders. Storms, droughts, and other natural events were often blamed on witchcraft. So were accidents, injuries, and illnesses. Even doctors agreed that some diseases were caused by witchcraft.

The Puritans had brought their ideas about witchcraft from England to the New World. They believed that witches made a deal with the Devil. A witch signed the Devil's black book, and the Devil put a mark on the witch's body.

The Devil granted a witch's wishes in return for his or her soul. The witch collected more souls for the Devil by tormenting innocent people until they too added their names to the Devil's book. In this way, the Devil used witches to wage war against God, heaven, and the church.

To the Puritans, however, the Devil was more than the enemy of heaven and earth. He was their particular enemy. The Puritans believed that their religion was the purest. Their community was based strictly on the Bible and was committed to be free from sin. For this reason, the Devil posed a special threat to the Puritans. Every man, woman, and child had to fight a personal battle against Satan's evil.

People feared witches because they were agents of the Devil and had the power to do harmful magic. Witches could cast spells. They could ruin a farmer's crops or cause farm animals to die. They could make people sick, kill babies, and burn down houses.

In some ways, witchcraft practices were the opposite of the Puritan faith. The Puritans attended church, where they worshiped God. Witches were thought to assemble in forests or caves or on mountains on moonlit nights. At these meetings, or *sabbaths,* they worshiped the Devil. Witches said prayers backwards instead of forwards. While some church services used white bread, witchcraft ceremonies used bread that was black or red. Instead of the respectful quiet of a church, witches' sabbaths had wild dancing, singing, and feasting. Afterwards, it was said, the witches returned home as they had come—riding on broomsticks.

As talk of witchcraft spread through Salem Village, the people saw a real and growing danger in their midst. Year after year, ministers had urged them to beware. In their fiery sermons,

Reverend Parris and others had warned against the Devil and his tricks.

The ministers had indeed been right. Satan had come to Salem Village.

Chapter 5

By the end of February, Salem's people had more reason than ever to be afraid. No longer was it only the young cousins who were bewitched. Now there were others.

First, twelve-year-old Ann Putnam began showing signs of bewitchment just like Betty and Abigail. Ann came from one of the leading families of Salem Village. She was a smart but high-strung girl with an active imagination. Ann often seemed very mature in thought and manner. But she was only a year older than her close friend Abigail and much younger than many of her other friends.

Not long after Ann started acting bewitched, seventeen-year-old Elizabeth Hubbard did the same. Elizabeth was an orphan. She lived with the Griggs family as their servant. Soon, two other teenagers, Mercy Lewis (a servant of the Putnams) and Mary Walcott, joined them.

All these girls had often visited the parsonage. They, too, had taken part in forbidden games. Then they had watched in horror as Betty and Abigail began having awful fits. And then, suddenly, they also started to behave strangely. They cried out. They dropped to the floor and made strange sounds. Their bodies twisted and stiffened. They choked and babbled.

Today, psychiatrists would label the girls' behavior *hysteria*. In 1692, people called it witchcraft.

Reverend Parris was horrified. So were the families and friends of the newly afflicted girls. Fear swept the village like an icy wind.

The number of afflicted girls was growing. The Devil himself seemed to be attacking Salem Village.

"It's said that Elizabeth Booth is bewitched," someone whispered.

"John Proctor's servant girl Mary Warren, too."

"Abigail Hobbs and Susannah Sheldon as well."

"Surely Satan is among us!"

Like Betty and Abigail, some of the other afflicted girls also said they saw visions. They too named Tituba.

More questions and charges were hurled against the frightened slave. Reverend Parris was especially hard on her. He shouted at Tituba. He even beat her to get her to confess.

But the slave still denied that she was a witch. "I did no harm to anyone," she said, weeping.

Reverend Parris was desperate. His home, his congregation, the whole village was in an uproar. He questioned the afflicted girls again and again. He was determined to find out who had bewitched them. Others joined the minister in his questioning. Thomas Putnam, Ann Putnam's father, was one. He was an important man in Salem Village and a close ally of the minister.

As the afflicted girls were questioned, they cried and screamed and had more fits. But Reverend Parris and the others would not give up.

"Who is it?" they demanded. "Who afflicts thee?"

Again the girls named Tituba. But this was not enough. The slave would not confess, and the people of Salem Village were becoming more and more frightened. The harsh questioning only made the girls more afraid. They wept and tried to hide their faces. But there was no escape.

"We must drive the Devil from Salem!" Reverend Parris thundered. His face was red. "Tell us who afflicts thee! Who? Who?"

Finally, the girls choked out two other names.
Sarah Good.
Sarah Osborne
Reverend Parris and Thomas Putnam looked at each other. These two names came as no sur-

prise to either man, nor to anyone else. Both Sarah Good and Sarah Osborne were disliked in Salem Village. Both women were often gossiped about.

Sarah Good was bad tempered and troublesome. Her husband rarely worked. Sarah went about town muttering, grumbling, and smoking her pipe. She begged for food for herself and her ragged little children. But she did not seem at all grateful for any charity she received.

Sarah Osborne was different. But she was no more popular than Sarah Good. She was a quarrelsome and sickly older woman. Her reputation was questionable. Among other things, she was said to have lived in sin with one of her servants.

Now, not just Tituba, but *three* women had been named. Village leaders acted at once.

Thomas Putnam, his brother Edward, and two other men made out a formal complaint. They charged Tituba, Sarah Good, and Sarah Osborne with using witchcraft to harm Betty and Abigail, Ann Putnam, and Elizabeth Hubbard.

The three accused women were arrested without delay. Their hearings would begin on March 1. If there was enough evidence, a formal trial would follow. If found guilty, the women would suffer the legal penalty for witchcraft.

That penalty was death.

Chapter 6

The fear that erupted in Salem Village had been brewing for years. The villagers had been under great stress.

Smallpox epidemics had taken a heavy toll. Many people had died. Others had watched their babies and children die. Some Puritans said that smallpox was a punishment from God. They believed that even a few sinners could bring punishment to the whole village.

The Puritans also faced the constant threat of Indian raids. Indeed, it was rumored that the Indians would soon launch a major attack. People living in Salem's widely scattered farmhouses worried about defending themselves. As always, farmers kept their guns close by.

There were other worries, too. In 1684 England had revoked Massachusetts' charter as a colony. No new charter had as yet been established. Without a charter, the people had no legal rights to their farms or land.

Added to these concerns was the preachers' constant talk of the Devil and hellfire. The well-known Boston minister Cotton Mather described in frightening words Satan's "army of evil spirits." Other ministers warned that people were not as religious or respectful as they should be. In their sermons, they spoke of the Devil's power to tempt and deceive. They told how Satan and his agents fooled people by taking different shapes.

To the Puritans, it felt as though enemies—visible and invisible—were everywhere. In this climate of fear and tension, charges of witchcraft set off a witch hunt like a spark igniting a blaze.

On the morning of March 1, 1692, an excited crowd gathered in Salem Village. It seemed as if the whole village had come to attend the hearings of Tituba, Sarah Good, and Sarah Osborne.

Two magistrates, or judges, walked down the road toward the meetinghouse. The crowd buzzed at how impressive the men looked. They wore fine clothes. They had on long black cloaks and black felt hats. Walking with the magistrates were their assistants and various local officials.

Next came the constables with the prisoners. All three women had their hands bound in chains. Tituba walked in silence, looking scared.

Sarah Good frowned and grumbled. Sarah Osborne looked weak and sick. At times she stumbled and nearly fell.

Behind the prisoners walked Thomas Putnam and the other men who had filed charges. They were dressed in their best clothes. They looked and acted important. Talking quietly with Thomas Putnam was Reverend Parris.

The four afflicted girls named in the complaint came next. Abigail Williams and Ann Putnam were first. They glanced nervously around at the crowd. Everyone was looking at them. Behind Abigail and Ann were Betty Parris and Elizabeth Hubbard. Both girls were pale. They kept their eyes down as they walked.

The magistrates entered the meetinghouse. They walked to the front and took seats at a long table, facing the room. The other people followed them in, except the prisoners. They were kept outside until the magistrates sent for them.

The meetinghouse was soon packed. People filled the rows of wooden benches. They sat in the aisles. They stood in the back of the room. They squeezed in anywhere they could. No one wanted to miss this event.

It was winter, and there was no heat in the meetinghouse. But the people were crammed so closely together and their excitement was so great that no one spoke of the cold.

Seats in the front were saved for the afflicted girls. Space was also set aside between the first row of spectators and the magistrates' table. The accused women would stand in this space.

Reverend Parris came up. He stood at his pulpit. It was from here that the minister had so often preached about evil and the Devil. The crowd quieted down at once.

Reverend Parris said a prayer. He asked for God's strength and guidance. Then he stepped down and let the magistrates take over.

The magistrates were John Hathorne and Jonathan Corwin. Both were important and successful men. They had traveled from Salem Town to run the hearings.

John Hathorne asked most of the questions. He was supposed to be fair and impartial, but his point of view was clear. Hathorne had come to Salem Village expecting to find witches and the Devil at work. It was plain from the start that he thought the accused were guilty. Hathorne wasn't looking for innocence. He wanted confessions.

"Bring in the first prisoner," the magistrate ordered.

Two constables led in Sarah Good. She muttered angrily as she walked to the front. She stood before the magistrates' long table, looking ragged and dirty. She scowled at Hathorne and Corwin.

The four afflicted girls named in the complaint were also brought up to the magistrates' table. They stood close together, trying to gain courage from one another.

"Do not look at the prisoner," Hathorne told them.

The room became silent.

Hathorne stared at Sarah Good. She stared right back. She resented the way she was being treated and wanted the magistrate to know it.

Hathorne straightened in his chair.

"Sarah Good," he said in a loud, clear voice, "what evil spirit have you associated with?"

"None," she shot back.

"Have you not made a contract with the Devil?" Hathorne demanded. His cold gaze was fixed on her.

The magistrate glanced at the afflicted girls. They lowered their eyes, frightened. Then he looked again at the accused woman.

"Why do you hurt these children, Sarah Good?"

"I do *not* hurt them."

"If not you, then who do you use to hurt them?"

"I use nobody. I do not hurt these children."

"What creature do you use?"

"*No* creature," she said angrily. "This charge is false!"

Hathorne's eyes narrowed. "I ask you again, have you not made a contract with the Devil?"

"And I say again, no."

The magistrate paused. A stubborn woman, he thought. How would he show her guilt?

After a moment, Hathorne turned to the

afflicted girls. They all avoided his eyes. Betty looked as if she might cry.

"Children, I ask you now to look upon this woman." The girls hesitated. They were scared and confused. "Is this the person who is hurting you?"

Slowly, one by one, the girls looked at Sarah Good. They felt all eyes in the room staring at them. The crowd was listening, waiting. The two magistrates were waiting, too. And Reverend Parris. And Thomas Putnam. And all the other important men in the room.

The girls felt they could hardly breathe. Very softly, Betty began to sob. Abigail took her hand. Then she started crying, too.

Sarah Good glared at the girls. She muttered something under her breath.

"Is this the person who is hurting you?" Hathorne repeated. His voice was loud and hard.

"Yes," Ann Putnam said, and she too began to cry.

Abigail glanced at her. Then she nodded. "Yes," she said.

Then Betty and Elizabeth Hubbard both nodded. "Yes," they agreed.

Suddenly, Ann shrieked and fell to the floor. Then Betty screamed. Then Abigail. In an instant, all four girls were on the floor shouting and crying. Their heads and bodies jerked and twisted this way and that. They made choking sounds.

"Witchcraft!" someone shouted. "Lord preserve us!"

The room exploded with shouts and screams. Some people covered their faces in terror. A few ran from the meetinghouse. Several fainted. Others began to pray.

Many people rushed to help the girls. But the girls just kept crying and shouting and rolling about on the floor.

"Sarah Good, do you not see now what you have done?" Hathorne shouted over all the noise. "Why do you not tell us the truth? Why do you torment these poor children?"

"I do not torment them," Sarah Good replied. She stared at the four girls. She was shocked.

"Who do you use to hurt them?"

"I use nobody," she insisted, scarcely believing her eyes.

"Then how are these children being tormented?"

Sarah Good didn't know what to say. She watched the girls having fits and shook her head. She was as distressed as anyone else by what she was seeing.

"What do *I* know of this?" she said. "You brought others to the meetinghouse, but you charge me."

Hathorne leaned forward. "Do you mean to say that these others are responsible?"

Sarah Good felt trapped. If these girls were truly bewitched, it was not her doing. Someone else must indeed be to blame.

"Who is responsible?" Hathorne pressed her. "Which of the others? Who torments these children?"

Sarah Good looked about. She muttered to herself.

"Who torments these children?" Hathorne repeated.

"Osborne," she said finally. "It was Sarah Osborne."

Hathorne leaned back in his chair. He spoke quietly with Jonathan Corwin. The other magistrate nodded.

Sarah Good had not yet confessed. But the magistrates had gotten enough from her for now.

Hathorne asked a few more questions. Then he ordered Sarah Good to be taken out.

"Bring in Sarah Osborne," the magistrate said.

Chapter 7

The constables removed Sarah Good from the meetinghouse. Immediately, the afflicted girls quieted down. All four were helped up from the floor. They straightened their clothing. Then they took the seats that had been saved for them.

Abigail and Ann Putnam whispered to each other. Betty sniffled and wiped tears from her cheeks. Elizabeth Hubbard sat in silence, looking down at her hands.

The meetinghouse buzzed. People talked about the afflicted girls. They told stories about Sarah Good and spoke of casting spells and witchcraft. They wondered aloud if Sarah Osborne was as guilty as Sarah Good.

They would soon find out. The constables brought in Sarah Osborne. She walked unsteadily to the front, looking dazed. She stopped before the magistrates' table. Recent illness had left her very pale.

Hathorne began with the same questions he had asked Sarah Good. Sarah Osborne, too, denied that she had hurt the children or made a contract with the Devil.

Hathorne paused, watching her.

"Are you acquainted with Sarah Good?" he asked.

"I know who she is," she said slowly. "It has been two years since I have seen her."

"Sarah Good says that it is you who hurts these children."

She frowned. "I hurt no children. If the Devil takes for himself my appearance, I know nothing of this."

Hathorne looked at the afflicted girls.

"Children, I ask you to stand."

The girls rose to their feet.

"Look upon this woman," Hathorne said. "Do you know her?"

The girls all nodded.

"Is this one of the persons who hurts you?"

"Yes," Abigail said.

"Yes," Ann Putnam agreed.

And before Betty or Elizabeth Hubbard even had a chance to speak, Abigail and Ann cried out and collapsed. An instant later, the other two girls did the same. Then all four girls began twisting around on the floor, screaming and crying and choking.

Sarah Osborne gasped. "This is not of my doing! More likely someone would bewitch me than I would bewitch anyone!"

"You say you are bewitched?" Hathorne asked loudly over the noise of the afflicted girls.

"No, I only—"

"Come, then," Hathorne said impatiently. "By your own word, you speak of bewitchment."

"No, I—"

"You are bewitched, or you bewitch others?"

She shook her head. She was bewildered.

"Tell us, then," Hathorne pressed. "Which is it?"

"No . . . I . . . well, one time I was frightened—"

"Frightened by what?"

"I was asleep. Or . . . I think I was asleep."

"What frightened you?" Hathorne demanded.

"I saw . . . think I saw . . . maybe I dreamed . . ."

"What?"

"A thing . . . like a man . . . all black. And it pinched and pulled at me."

"Have you spoken with the Devil?" Hathorne asked.

"No."

"Has the Devil tempted you?"

"No."

"Yet, I am told that you do not come to church service. Is that not the Devil's doing?"

Sarah Osborne rubbed her eyes. She felt dizzy.

"I have been sick. I could not go to church. I have never seen the Devil."

"But you say you have seen a black 'thing like a man.'"

"I . . ." She hesitated. She looked around for help. But there was no one to help her.

"Enough then," Hathorne said. He turned to the constables. "Take her out," he ordered. "Bring in Tituba."

Chapter 8

All those inside the meetinghouse had been shocked by what they had seen and heard. But Tituba's words would shock them even more.

The slave looked terrified as she walked to the front of the room. Day after day, Reverend Parris and others had continued to question her. They shouted at her. They threatened all sorts of punishments. The minister beat her. He called her an evil creature, a servant of the Devil. Tituba had cried. She had pleaded her innocence. But they would not leave her alone.

As soon as they saw Tituba, the afflicted girls began having terrible fits. Hathorne had not even asked a question yet! But the crowd was not surprised. Everyone knew that the slave had been the first person to be accused.

Tituba stood helplessly before the magistrates' table. She winced at the girls' awful cries and howls. She lowered her head in despair.

Hathorne started to question her. At first, Tituba tried again to deny the charges. She said she had not hurt the children. She said she had not talked with the Devil.

But Hathorne shot question after question at her. Many of the questions were the same ones Tituba had answered time and again for Reverend Parris and others. Her answers had gained her nothing in the past. Nothing but shouts, threats, and beatings. She knew they would gain her nothing now either. It was no use.

"Have you associated with the Devil?" Hathorne demanded again. "Tell the truth! Who hurts these children? Is it you? Is it the Devil?"

Tituba just shook her head. Tears ran down her cheeks.

"Who is it? *Speak!*"

"Maybe it is the Devil," Tituba said at last.

"Ah! So you know it is the Devil!" Hathorne said loudly. "In what form does he come? How does he look when he hurts the children?"

Tituba shut her eyes. Her mind was racing. The questions would never stop. These men would never let her be. They would never believe her. They would keep after her and after her and after her. Unless . . . unless she told them what they wanted to hear.

"He . . . he looks like a man."

"So you *have* seen the Devil!"

All of a sudden, the room quieted. Everyone

was listening, even the afflicted girls.

"He came to me," Tituba said. "A tall man. In black. He wanted me to serve him."

"So you hurt the children?"

"Not I."

"Who then?"

"Four women."

"Who?"

"Sarah Osborne. Sarah Good. I do not know the others."

"And you? Did you not hurt the children?"

Tituba had been asked this question a hundred times. She knew they would keep asking it until she gave them the answer they wanted.

She looked at the magistrate. "Yes . . . I hurt them. But only once," she added quickly. "And I will not hurt them more."

People were whispering to one another. Several called out for God's protection.

"Why did you hurt them?" Hathorne pressed.

"Sarah Osborne and Sarah Good said that I must. They said if I did not, they would hurt *me*. I was afraid."

Tituba then described how she had gone to Dr. Griggs' home, where Elizabeth Hubbard lived, and to the home of the Putnam family. She told how she had been forced to pinch both Elizabeth and Ann.

The murmuring in the meetinghouse grew louder. Tituba's words were chilling. But the slave had even more startling things to say.

She began to speak of strange creatures she had seen. Creatures of the Devil. She described a great black dog. A red cat. A yellow bird. A thing that had wings and a woman's face.

People in the room nodded. Everyone knew that witches were served by evil spirits called "familiars." Familiars often took the shape of animals. They helped witches harm their victims.

A familiar fed off a witch's blood. Accused witches were commonly searched for a "witch's mark." This mark—usually just a mole or birthmark—supposedly showed the spot from where a familiar sucked blood. When Tituba spoke of the yellow bird, she said that it sucked from a place between Sarah Good's fingers.

The more questions Hathorne asked, the more details Tituba gave. The magistrates listened to every word she said. They were as fascinated as everyone else in the meetinghouse.

Tituba was glad to be speaking. It was a relief to have people listening to her instead of shouting at her. If they wanted tales of the Devil, she would give them tales of the Devil. She was very good at telling stories.

"And when you went to torment the children, how did you go?" Hathorne asked.

Tituba thought a moment. "Upon a stick," she answered. "We rode upon a stick."

Another wave of whispers swept over the crowd.

"All of you?" the magistrate asked.

The slave nodded. "We took hold of one another. Good and Osborne behind me."

Hathorne glanced at the other magistrate. Jonathan Corwin was busily taking notes. Hathorne could well understand why.

Tituba went on and on. By day's end, she was tired. She hoped that the magistrates would now be done with her.

But they were not.

"Take Tituba to the jail," Hathorne told the constables. "And the other two prisoners with her. We will speak more with all three."

Tituba shook her head wearily. It seemed that her nightmare would never end.

And Salem's had just begun.

Chapter 9

The hearings of Tituba, Sarah Good, and Sarah Osborne went on for several days. Tituba told more disturbing stories of witches, familiars, and "the tall man in black." Sarah Good shouted and grumbled. "You have no true evidence!" she snarled at the magistrates. Sarah Osborne said over and over that she was innocent.

Meanwhile, worry and suspicion were infecting Salem Village like a sickness. Tituba's words in particular had fueled people's fears. At one point, the slave had talked about the Devil's book:

"The tall man showed me the book," she said. "I put a mark in it. A red mark. Like blood. I saw nine marks in the book," she added. One was Sarah Good's. One was Sarah Osborne's.

Nine marks, Tituba had said. But she could identify only two. *Who made the other marks?* everyone wanted to know. Who else signed the

Devil's book? What other witches are walking among us? Perhaps a friend or neighbor? Maybe even a cousin or uncle?

No one was safe. Witches could work their evil anywhere. Had they not entered the Putnams' home and afflicted both young Ann and the servant Mercy Lewis? And Dr. Griggs' servant Elizabeth? And John Proctor's Mary Warren? *Had witches not invaded the very home of the minister himself?*

Adding to the villagers' fears was the idea of "shapes" or "specters." The Puritans believed that witches could send their ghostlike spirits out to harm people. A witch could be in one place, while the witch's shape or specter tormented a victim somewhere else. When Betty and Abigail first said that Tituba had pinched them and stuck them with invisible pins, the girls meant Tituba's specter.

As talk of witches and victims grew, the line between specters and people faded. Thus, if a man claimed—or imagined or even just dreamed—that Sarah Good had hurt him, Sarah Good the *person* might be blamed for witchcraft. Few people stopped to ask a key question: Couldn't the Devil use the specters of innocent people to do his evil? If so, those innocent people would be blamed for the deeds of specters outside their control!

As the hearings went on, people's fears stirred their imagination. They began seeing witches, specters, and odd creatures every-where. One man said that Tituba and Sarah Osborne had mysteriously appeared and disap-peared along a dark road. Another man saw Sarah Good in his bedroom. Other people reported strange dogs and cats.

The hearings finally ended on March 5. Hathorne and Corwin were satisfied. There was more than enough evidence against Sarah Good and Sarah Osborne. Both women would go on trial for witchcraft. As for Tituba, she had con-fessed. She probably would not be tried. Still, the magistrates had to decide what to do with her. In the meantime, she too would remain a prisoner.

Two days later, Sarah Good, Sarah Osborne, and Tituba were taken, in chains, to Boston jail. With these three gone, the people of Salem Village prayed that the afflicted girls would recover. They prayed that the witchcraft scare had passed.

But their prayers went unanswered. The girls' fits continued. Indeed, sometimes they were worse than before.

Chapter 10

Not long after the hearings, Reverend Parris and his wife made a decision. They would send young Betty away from Salem Village.

When not having fits, most of the afflicted girls seemed well enough. But not Betty. She was getting worse, both physically and mentally. Betty looked thin and pale. She cried often. She babbled about witches and Satan. She screamed in her sleep.

Perhaps Betty suffered most because she was the youngest. No one knew for sure. But staying in Salem Village was clearly doing her no good at all. So, Reverend and Mrs. Parris sent their daughter to live with another family in Salem Town. Her cousin Abigail remained.

Interestingly, once Betty Parris left the village, she did indeed get better. Maybe it was being away from Abigail, Ann, and the other girls. Maybe it was living outside the tense atmosphere of Salem Village. Maybe it was the fact that Betty finally confessed to having played forbidden fortune-telling games. Whatever the reason, Betty very slowly did begin to recover.

Meanwhile, the other girls stayed in Salem Village. They spent time together in one another's homes and in the meetinghouse. Ministers, town leaders, and many others spoke with them daily about witchcraft. People whispered and pointed when the girls walked by. And everyone gasped and drew back whenever the girls went into their awful fits.

On March 11, Reverend Parris led a day of fasting and prayer. The minister had done this before, hoping to fight off the Devil. For this day, Reverend Parris also invited ministers from other towns.

As before, fasting and prayer did not help. The girls even had fits during the prayer services. The ministers all shook their heads. Would the situation in Salem Village never improve? they asked themselves.

In fact, the situation got worse. Ann Putnam began complaining of yet another witch. She accused a woman named Martha Corey of tormenting her.

This accused witch was very different from Tituba, Sarah Good, and Sarah Osborne. Martha Corey was a strong, intelligent, well-spoken, respectable member of the church. She was married to Giles Corey, a well-to-do farmer.

Edward Putnam volunteered to question her. He was Ann's uncle, brother of Thomas Putnam. He was one of the men who had filed the complaint against the other accused witches. Edward would take with him another respected villager, Ezekiel Cheever.

Chapter 11

Martha Corey had seen and done many things in her sixty-five years. Not much surprised her anymore. So when Edward Putnam and Ezekiel Cheever came to her house one Saturday, she smiled at them.

"I've heard the talk," she said, letting them in. "So it's me you've come to accuse now, is it?"

Martha Corey was known as a woman who spoke her mind. Putnam and Cheever had expected her to be direct. What they had not expected was her light tone.

True, Martha Corey had been one of the few people not to attend the hearings of Sarah Good, Sarah Osborne, and Tituba. But surely she understood the dangers that Salem Village was facing. Friends and neighbors would have given her an earful. So would her husband, Giles. He had gone to the hearings despite his wife's protests. He was as stubborn as she.

"This is a serious matter, Goody Corey," Putnam told her. "A most serious matter." "Goody" was short for "Goodwife." Puritans referred to one another as "Goodwife" and "Goodman." "Mr." and "Mrs." were more formal titles, usually used for important people.

Martha laughed, which made Putnam and Cheever frown.

"I am not a witch," she said.

"Yet you are so accused."

"By a child." Martha looked amused at the thought.

"You are a church member, Goody Corey," Putnam said. "It does no honor to the church or to God to be so accused."

"I cannot help what another person says."

"Three women before you already stand accused," Cheever said.

"So I have heard." She looked from one man to the other. "I doubt there are any witches."

"You doubt there are witches?" Putnam said, shocked. Everyone knew that witches were as real as the Devil himself.

"I doubt there are witches in Salem."

"Three are in prison, Goody Corey!" Putnam said.

Martha smiled. "If any three were witches, those three might well be. They are often up to no good. But I go to church. I am faithful to God. I am no witch."

"Even a witch may go to church," Cheever said.

Martha's smile faded. She was losing patience. "Look not to me for witchcraft," she told them. "Look instead to the wagging tongues that do Devil's work in Salem!"

Putnam and Cheever glanced at each other. They disliked Martha's manner as much as her words.

"Good day, Goody Corey," Putnam said coldly. With that, both men turned and walked out of the house.

Martha Corey shook her head. "Foolishness," she muttered to herself. Then she closed the door after them.

Martha tried to put the matter out of her mind. But Putnam and Cheever's visit did not sit well with her. She had liked their tone no more than they had liked hers.

I have better things to do now, Martha thought, than waste time on such silliness. Spring is almost upon us. All the snow will soon be gone. We need to prepare for plowing and planting. Yet, I cannot let such loose words hang in the air.

The following Monday, Martha Corey set out for the Putnam home. She wanted to speak with the child who had accused her. Perhaps she could talk some sense into the girl.

But the situation was far more difficult than Martha had thought. As soon as she began speaking to Ann Putnam, the girl screamed. She fled across the room and dropped to her knees. She babbled about yellow birds and cried out for her mother. She moaned and wept and made choking noises.

Mercy Lewis came running in. Mercy was the Putnams' seventeen-year-old servant. She saw Ann in the midst of her terrible fit. She looked at Martha Corey. Then, a moment later, Mercy too was on the floor, having a fit of her own.

There was nothing Martha could do. She left the screaming girls and returned home.

A few days later, Martha received another shock. She learned that now Ann Putnam's *mother,* Thomas Putnam's wife, was claiming that Martha's specter was tormenting her.

Martha knew that Goody Putnam was a troubled woman. Some years earlier, Goody Putnam's sister and her sister's three children had all died. Goody Putnam had never been the same. Yet, Martha had never expected that Goody Putnam, like her daughter and her servant, would become one of the afflicted "girls."

Less than a week passed before Edward Putnam and another man filed a formal complaint against Martha Corey. They accused her of using witchcraft to harm Thomas Putnam's wife, daughter, and servant. They also accused her of hurting Abigail Williams and Elizabeth Hubbard.

The next Saturday, March 19, a warrant was issued for the arrest of Martha Corey.

Chapter 12

The same day that the warrant for Martha Corey was issued, Reverend Deodat Lawson arrived from Boston. He had been the minister of Salem Village before Reverend Parris. Reverend Parris had invited him to observe the afflicted girls and offer any help he could.

Reverend Lawson went to his room at the inn to unpack. A short time later, seventeen-year-old Mary Walcott came by. Mary was one of the girls who used to listen to Tituba's stories with Betty and Abigail.

Although he hadn't seen her in several years, the minister remembered Mary at once. They spoke for a while. Then Mary started to leave. Suddenly, she let out a shriek.

"What is it, child?" Reverend Lawson asked, startled.

"Oh, I have been bitten!" Mary cried, holding her arm.

"Bitten?"

"By a specter!"

The minister picked up a candle and walked closer. He examined Mary's arm.

"Indeed," he said, frowning. "They do appear to be teeth marks."

Reverend Lawson was still puzzling over the red marks when he came to the Parris home that evening. He was about to discuss them with Reverend Parris when Abigail screamed.

Both ministers were taken aback. The girl had seemed fine just a moment ago. Now she was racing around, shouting, and flapping her arms.

Abruptly, she froze. She was staring straight ahead, her mouth open.

"Abigail?" Reverend Lawson said. "What is it? What do you see?"

"A specter!" she cried.

"Where?" Reverend Lawson's eyes searched the room.

"There she stands! Can you not see her?"

"Who?" Reverend Parris asked.

"Goody Nurse."

"Rebecca Nurse?" Reverend Lawson said, shocked. He remembered Rebecca Nurse very well. She was one of the kindest, most devout people in Salem. Many times had the minister heard the woman called a saint.

"She wants me to sign the book," Abigail said fearfully. "The *Devil's* book."

Reverend Lawson was speechless.

"Abigail—" Reverend Parris began, reaching a hand for her shoulder.

The girl jumped back from the invisible specter.

"*No!* I won't sign it! I *won't!*"

With that, Abigail dashed across the room.

Revered Lawson looked from the unseen specter to the wild-eyed girl. He didn't know what to think. He saw nothing, no one. Young girls did have powerful imaginations. But surely Abigail wasn't pretending. The poor child acted as though she were fleeing the Devil himself.

"May God have mercy . . . ," he whispered.

The next morning, Reverend Lawson was to lead Sunday services. He looked weary as he entered the meetinghouse. Thoughts of specters and demons had kept him awake much of the night.

From the pulpit, the minister looked out at the congregation. Seated together in one row were five of the afflicted girls: Abigail Williams, Ann Putnam, Mary Walcott, Elizabeth Hubbard, and Mercy Lewis. The girls sat still, like well-behaved children, all eyes fixed on him. They seemed well enough, the minister thought. But he felt a chill nonetheless.

Reverend Lawson heard a murmur from the back of the room. In walked Martha Corey. The warrant for her arrest had been issued late the day before. However, it could not be served on Sunday. So, for today at least, Goody Corey was still a free woman.

Martha had considered staying home. She realized that her coming to church would cause a stir, but she knew that she had done nothing wrong. She had no intention of missing Sunday services.

The girls grew restless as soon as they saw her. Several times during Reverend Lawson's service one or more of them cried out or interrupted the minister. Such behavior in church was more than rude. In Puritan society, it was shocking.

As the service went on, the afflicted girls' outbursts got worse. At times, the girls acted as strangely as they ever had. What's more, two women joined them: Bethshaa Pope and Sarah Bibber.

Reverend Lawson could scarcely continue. He had never seen anything like this.

Suddenly, Abigail Williams jumped up. She pointed to the wooden beam overhead.

"Look!" she cried. "Goody Corey sits upon the beam! Her yellow bird sucks from between her fingers!"

Everyone looked up. One or two people screamed, but no one else could see the specter.

The minister waited for the congregation to quiet down. Then he tried to go on with his sermon.

A few minutes later, it was Ann Putnam who interrupted.

"I see the yellow bird," she called.

Reverend Lawson paused, but neither Ann nor Abigail said anything more. The minister completed his sermon, relieved that there were no more outbursts.

When services were over, Martha Corey rose and calmly left the meetinghouse. She heard the people's whispers, but she ignored them.

I'll show them all tomorrow, Martha thought. Her hearing on charges of witchcraft was scheduled for the next day. Like the three accused before her, Martha Corey would be questioned by John Hathorne and Jonathan Corwin.

Chapter 13

On Monday morning, the meetinghouse was again filled to overflowing. The magistrates sat behind their long table. Seated with them was Reverend Parris. He would write down all that was said. Also present was the minister from Salem Town, Nicholas Noyes. The afflicted girls sat in the front row.

Reverend Noyes came up to the pulpit to say the opening prayer. He was a portly man in his forties. He asked for the Lord's help in the fight against the Devil. Then John Hathorne and Jonathan Corwin took over.

As before, Hathorne did most of the questioning. His manner was stern. Three accused witches were already in prison. Hathorne had no doubt that there would soon be a fourth.

The constables brought in Martha Corey. She smiled confidently. I'll put an end to this nonsense, she thought. I'll tell these magistrates I'm no witch, and that will be that.

But Martha had misjudged the situation. As Edward Putnam had warned her when he came to her house, this was a most serious matter. Martha believed that her innocence was enough to protect her. She thought the magistrates would have to prove that she was a witch. Instead, the magistrates left it to Martha to prove that she *wasn't*. As Martha Corey and other accused persons soon learned, doing so was impossible.

Hathorne lost no time beginning his attack.

"Why do you hurt these children?" he demanded.

Before Martha could even answer, the afflicted girls began having fits. They screamed and twisted in their seats. Several fell to the floor.

"Why do you hurt these children?" Hathorne repeated more loudly.

The noise from the girls made it hard for Martha even to think. Her confidence was shaken.

"I would like to say a prayer, if I may," Martha said.

"You are not here to pray, Goody Corey. You are here to answer charges."

"If I may, I only want to—"

"You may *not*," Hathorne cut her off. "Tell us why you hurt these children."

"I am innocent. I have nothing to do with witchcraft. I go to church. I am faithful to God."

"Witch!" one of the afflicted girls yelled.

"Witch! Witch!" the others began to shout.

Martha drew back. She stared at the girls. She could hardly believe what was happening.

Hathorne fired more questions at her. Martha answered as best she could. Again and again, she said she was innocent.

The girls' fits only got worse.

"Her specter is biting me!" Ann Putnam cried.

"She is choking me!" screamed Abigail Williams.

"She is pinching me!" howled another girl.

"Help me!"

"Take her off me!"

All the while, Martha stood gaping at them. There was nothing she could do.

"I am innocent," she repeated. Few people heard.

Suddenly, Abigail pointed her finger at Martha.

"Look!"

The girls quieted down. They all looked where Abigail was pointing.

Hathorne frowned. "What do you see, child?"

"A man," Abigail said. "He is whispering in her ear!"

"Yes," Mary Walcott agreed. "I see him too."

At that, the afflicted girls resumed their awful crying and wailing. Goody Pope and Goody Bibber also joined in.

Martha shook her head. They've all lost their senses, she thought. They're all *mad*.

"What did the man whisper to you?" Hathorne asked.

Martha stared at the magistrate. How could he take the girls' word without so much as a doubt?

"We must not believe everything these children say," she said.

Hathorne ignored her.

"Tell us what the man whispered," he said.

"I saw no man," Martha replied.

"Did you not hear his words?"

"No. I heard nothing."

The afflicted girls screamed and moaned even more loudly. Their frightful cries echoed through the meetinghouse. Many of them rolled on the floor in a hysterical frenzy. Their bodies twisted horribly. Arms and legs waved this way and that. The girls' tongues hung out of their mouths. Two girls began bleeding from the mouth.

Several people jumped up to help the girls. Spectators were talking loudly among themselves.

Martha watched the whole scene with horror.

Hathorne raised his voice above the commotion.

"Confess!" he demanded.

"I am innocent."

"Look upon these afflicted persons. Do you think you can hide from the truth? Confess!"

"We must not believe these troubled children," Martha said bravely. But there was a note of fear in her voice now. Martha knew that her situation was desperate.

All of a sudden, a man in the sixth row rose to his feet. "I have evidence!" he shouted. He said that he'd seen Goody Corey threaten the afflicted girls. Martha denied the charge. But then three or four others in the crowd yelled that it was true.

Martha threw up her hands. "What can I say to so many false voices?"

"You can confess," Hathorne answered. He did not doubt her guilt. But if he could get an outright confession, that would be the strongest evidence of all.

Martha met the magistrate's eyes.

"And so I would—if I were guilty."

But Hathorne would not stop.

Meanwhile, the afflicted girls continued their fits. Worse, now they were reacting to Martha's every movement. If Martha squeezed her fingers together, the girls yelled that she was pinching them. If Martha bit her lip, they yelled that she was biting them. Before long, Martha was afraid to move at all.

"Who can doubt that Goody Corey is practicing witchcraft?" Reverend Nicholas Noyes called out. He was as eager as anyone to point the finger at witches. Reverend Parris nodded his head in agreement. So did Thomas Putnam.

Just then, Goody Pope screamed in pain. "She's tearing out my insides!" the woman shouted. With that, Goody Pope removed one of her shoes and flung it at Martha. It struck Martha in the head. She looked to the magistrates for some defense. But neither Hathorne nor Corwin said a word.

"All here are against me," Martha said in despair.

Hathorne tried yet again to get Martha to confess. Tired as she was after hours of questioning, Martha still refused. She looked the magistrate squarely in the eye.

"You cannot prove I am a witch," she told him.

But Hathorne had heard enough. He ordered Martha Corey taken to jail. She, too, would stand trial for witchcraft.

The magistrate leaned back in his chair. He felt satisfied. After all, he'd believed Martha Corey was guilty from the start.

Chapter 14

Martha Corey's hearing left the people of Salem feeling more uneasy than ever. She was a respectable church member. If she was a witch, then anyone could be one.

Adding to people's concerns was another fact. The number of afflicted persons was going up, not down. And not just girls were afflicted. Now even a few adults were seeing specters or having fits.

Of course, many of the afflicted persons were troubled even before the first whispers of witchcraft. Some were coping with the pressures of adolescence. Puritan strictness only added to their emotional stress. Others were feeling the effects of their past. Ann Putnam's mother, for example, had become unstable after the deaths of several family members. Night after night, the dead came to her in her dreams. Mercy Lewis was left an orphan when Indians killed her parents. Mary

Walcott's mother died when Mary was just a young child. Goody Bibber had for years been scorned as a gossip and a troublemaker.

Together, these girls and women fanned the flames of one another's affliction. Sometimes their frenzy even spread to other people around them.

Two days after Martha Corey went to jail, Reverend Deodat Lawson visited the Putnam home. The minister was still shaken by all that he'd seen since his arrival four days earlier. But Thomas Putnam had asked him to stop by. His wife's condition was serious enough to put her in bed.

Goody Putnam did indeed look weak and pale when Reverend Lawson saw her.

"What troubles you?" the minister asked.

"Not *what,* but *who,*" she replied. She described how for days Martha Corey had been hurting her. Then, once Goody Corey went to jail, Goody Nurse had begun to torment her.

"You're certain it is Goody Nurse?" Reverend Lawson asked. He still remembered his shock when Abigail had seen Rebecca Nurse's specter at the Parris home.

Goody Putnam said she had no doubt. Both her daughter Ann and her servant Mercy Lewis had also seen Goody Nurse. The minister was not surprised. He had heard that once one afflicted girl saw a specter, other girls soon reported seeing the same specter.

Goody Putnam asked the minister to pray with her. He did, but several times his prayers were interrupted by Goody Putnam's fits. At one point, she sat up and began shouting at the specter that tormented her.

"Be gone!" she cried. "Be gone, Goody Nurse! Why do you afflict me? What hurt did I ever do to you?"

As he had at the Parris home, Reverend Lawson searched the room for any sign of the specter. But he could see none.

The minister shook his head, troubled. He continued praying. Finally, Goody Putnam lay back on the bed. After a while, she seemed to rest more easily.

By the time he left the Putnam home, Reverend Lawson too was ready to believe that anyone could be a witch. But a gentle, elderly, faithful church member like Rebecca Nurse? It was hard to believe.

When he later heard the news, the minister was more saddened than surprised. A warrant had been issued for the arrest of Rebecca Nurse.

Chapter 15

Years later, people would still wonder how a woman like Rebecca Nurse could have been charged with witchcraft.

In her seventy-one years, Rebecca had won people's respect and affection. All her life, she had been a good and kind woman.

Still, not everyone in Salem Village viewed Rebecca Nurse as a saint. There were those who felt she and her husband Francis had been a little too prosperous.

Many years before, Francis made a deal to buy three hundred acres and a farmhouse from another family. He agreed to pay for the property over time. Such an arrangement is common today, but it was rare in the 1600s. Not everyone in the Puritan community approved.

Francis, Rebecca, and their many children and grandchildren worked hard. Year after year, they made payments. The land and house became theirs.

Some villagers admired the Nurses for what they had accomplished. But others resented the Nurses' good fortune.

"Old Francis is just a simple craftsman," Thomas Putnam once muttered. "He and his wife began with next to nothing. How can they have an estate such as this?" Others nodded in agreement. Maybe it was true. Maybe the Nurses had indeed risen a little above where they ought to be.

Thomas Putnam had another, more personal reason for feeling unkindly toward the Nurses. His family and theirs had a long history of land disagreements and had been arguing over boundary lines for many years.

Some people in Salem also disapproved of Rebecca because her mother had once been accused of witchcraft. She was never arrested, but gossip about her spread nonetheless. There were also whispers that witchery was passed on from parent to child.

Such gossip was stirred up again three years before the trials. Rebecca had a quarrel with her neighbors, the Holtons, who had let their hogs wander into Rebecca's garden. Rebecca lost her temper and shouted at both Sarah Holton and her husband Benjamin. Not long after, Benjamin died. Goody Holton blamed her husband's death on Rebecca. "The woman's a witch!" she declared to all who would listen.

Early on March 24, Rebecca Nurse was brought before the magistrates. The old woman had just gotten over an illness. She was still weak and pale and moved slowly.

The mood inside the meetinghouse was different from what it had been at previous hearings. The crowd was quieter. Many in the room were frowning. Some of Rebecca Nurse's relatives and friends cried when they saw her. People who had watched Tituba, Sarah Good, and the others with fear looked at Rebecca with fondness and sympathy.

The woman's frail appearance and humble manner touched even John Hathorne. He spoke more softly to her than he had to any of the other accused women. However, the magistrate found he had to raise his voice because Rebecca was partially deaf.

"I am innocent," Rebecca told him in answer to his usual questions about witchcraft and the Devil. "Before God, I say to you I am innocent."

"Goody Nurse," Hathorne went on, "Ann Putnam and Abigail Williams say you are hurting them. What do you reply to this?"

"I am innocent," Rebecca repeated. "I have never hurt a child." She shook her head. "Never in my life."

"Yet these two complain that you have."

"I have been ill," Rebecca said. "I have not even been out of my house for eight or nine days."

Rebecca did not understand that it did not matter if she had been sick in bed. Her *specter* could still be out and about.

But Hathorne looked uncertain. Could this soft-spoken, God-fearing old woman truly be a witch? Could she go about hurting children?

"You say you are innocent of this witchcraft ...," the magistrate said. It was as much a statement as a question. For the first time, people heard doubt in Hathorne's voice.

But before another word was spoken, Goody Putnam began to scream and choke. A moment later, the other girls joined her. Affliction was spreading like flames through a dry forest.

The two magistrates exchanged glances. The victims' fits grew louder, more frantic.

People in the crowd looked at one another. Their eyes widened with fear and suspicion. Who else in the room was a witch? And who would be the next victim?

Rebecca watched helplessly. The afflicted girls howled that she was biting and pinching them. Then, just as they had done with Martha Corey, the girls began reacting to every movement Rebecca made. When she tilted her head, the girls tilted their heads, too. But they moved their heads so far that it seemed their necks might break. Then they all screamed until Rebecca straightened up again.

Rebecca looked at the magistrates. But Hathorne and Corwin sat in silence. They may have wanted to believe that the old woman was innocent. But the frightful evidence against her was right before their eyes.

"What do you think of this?" Hathorne asked Rebecca when the noise had lessened somewhat.

Rebecca frowned. "I cannot tell what to think."

She raised her hand to her face. Immediately, all the afflicted girls raised their hands, too. Rebecca leaned back. The girls leaned back. Whatever movement she made, the girls imitated.

"Look!" Abigail burst out. She pointed at Rebecca just as she had pointed at Martha Corey. "A black man is whispering in her ear!"

"Yes, I see him," Ann Putnam quickly agreed.

Then Goody Putnam suddenly pointed to the window.

"The shape of Goody Nurse rides by the meetinghouse!" she cried. "She follows the black man!"

All the afflicted girls screamed that they saw the shapes too. The crowd saw nothing. But they were frightened. And the louder the afflicted girls screamed, the more frightened the people became.

"You brought the black man with you!" Goody Putnam shrieked at Rebecca. Then she collapsed to the floor. Her body began shaking. She made choking sounds.

"Witches among us!" someone shouted.

"Lord protect us!" yelled someone else.

"Cast out the Devil!" bellowed a third.

Thomas Putnam rushed to his wife's side. He lifted her from the floor and carried her out of the meetinghouse.

The crowd was in a frenzy. People were shouting and crying. They pointed at unseen terrors. The noise inside the meetinghouse was so loud that people outside, across the road, could hear it.

Rebecca raised her hand, as though to block out the awful scene. Immediately, the hands of all the afflicted girls shot into the air. Rebecca lowered her arm, and all the girls lowered theirs.

"Oh Lord, help me!" Rebecca pleaded.

"You would do well to confess," said Hathorne over the bedlam. In view of so much "evidence," the magistrate's doubts had faded.

Rebecca looked at him. "Would you have me lie?" she asked. The question was not asked lightly. Lying was a serious sin to the Puritans.

Hathorne studied her face. The old woman seemed upset. And yet, the magistrate could see no tears. Many women in the audience were crying. But Rebecca was not. Surely this was significant. It was well known that witches could not shed tears.

"Your eyes are dry," Hathorne said. "You see the pain these girls endure. Yet, you weep no tears."

Rebecca shook her head sadly. "You do not know what is in my heart."

Any hope of quiet in the room had long been lost. But Hathorne waited for the commotion to die down at least enough for his voice to be heard.

"Rebecca Nurse," he began. His face was grim. "Goody Putnam has sworn that the children of her sister died through bewitchment. She says it was you who caused their death."

Rebecca could hardly grasp the words she was hearing. She stared at the magistrate, unable to speak. She felt as if she were trapped in a nightmare.

Hathorne repeated the charge. "What say you to this?" He had to shout over the noise that had once again erupted throughout the meeting-house.

Rebecca thought carefully before she answered.

"The Devil may appear in my shape," she said.

She had raised an important point. If the Devil sent a specter to do evil without her knowledge, how could she be blamed?

But it was too late. The magistrates had already made up their minds.

Hathorne ordered the old woman taken to jail. Like Martha Corey and the others before her, Rebecca Nurse would go on trial for witchcraft.

Chapter 16

Rebecca Nurse was not the only person to face Hathorne and Corwin on March 24. A second accused witch was questioned after her, although far more briefly. Her name was Dorcas Good. She was Sarah Good's daughter.

Dorcas Good was four-and-a-half years old.

Looking back, it may be hard to imagine a small child brought before the magistrates. But in 1692, fear of Satan and witches had seized the people of Salem Village like a fever. If church members such as Rebecca Nurse and Martha Corey could be witches, then the Devil could claim anyone.

Perhaps, if little Dorcas had been the daughter of a respectable family, matters might have been different. But she was the child of Sarah Good. Ill-tempered, foul-mouthed Sarah Good. The pipe-smoking beggar, Sarah Good. The witch, Sarah Good.

Many people in the meetinghouse recognized the little girl. They had often seen her in the village. She was usually trailing behind her mother, just as ragged and dirty as she.

Dorcas looked no better today. Her clothes were soiled and torn. Her hair was unwashed and uncombed. Yet, with a little care, she would have been a pretty girl. Her dirt-streaked face was bright, and her eyes were as wide as any young girl's.

It was Ann Putnam and Mercy Lewis who had first accused Dorcas. Her specter was pinching and biting them, they said. People had some doubts. True, Dorcas was the daughter of an accused witch. It was also true that the girl sometimes ran about wildly, shouting or crying. But, after all, she was just a child.

Soon several other afflicted girls spoke out against Dorcas. With a growing number of voices crying witchcraft, people began to wonder. If a saintly grandmother like Rebecca Nurse was suspect, then why not a child? Especially Sarah Good's child. So little Dorcas Good was brought in for questioning.

Now, inside the meetinghouse, the girl looked curiously around. So many people. Why were they all looking at her? Who were these men behind the long table?

When her eyes stopped a moment on Ann Putnam, Ann instantly cried out. One or two other afflicted girls then did the same.

"She is hurting us!" Ann told Hathorne. The other girls agreed.

Dorcas frowned. She didn't understand.

Hathorne asked the little girl only a few questions. She was too young to grasp most of what he said.

The two magistrates conferred. Then Hathorne ordered Dorcas taken to the Salem prison along with Rebecca Nurse. He would question the child further there, he said, away from the distractions of the meetinghouse.

Two days later, Hathorne and Corwin visited Dorcas in her jail cell. The little girl was crying when they arrived. She hated the dark, cold, smelly cell with its damp stone walls. "I want to get out," she told the magistrates.

Hathorne explained that they had to ask her some questions. Dorcas tried to answer their strange questions. When she was uncertain, the magistrates offered suggestions. Their suggestions and the young girl's imagination helped the magistrates collect the information they had come for.

When Hathorne asked Dorcas if she had a familiar, maybe an animal, the girl nodded her head.

"A little snake," she said.

"And does your little snake sometimes take blood from you?"

She hesitated, then nodded again.

"From where does it take it?"

The girl thought a moment. Then she raised one finger. She pointed to a tiny red spot.

Hathorne and Corwin looked at each other. They were thinking the same thought. The red spot must be the witch's mark they had suspected.

"And who gave you this snake?"

Dorcas looked from one magistrate to the other. She shrugged.

"Don't know."

"Did a black man give it to you?" Hathorne suggested.

Dorcas shook her head. "No."

"Then who?"

She frowned.

"Come, now. Tell us who gave you the snake."

"My mother," Dorcas replied. "My mother gave me it."

Nearly two weeks passed before Dorcas finally left the Salem prison. She had lost weight, and her skin had paled. But she was happy to be free.

She squinted at the sunlight as the constable led her from the jail. He mounted a horse and pulled Dorcas up behind him. Together they rode off.

They traveled for hours. Dorcas didn't know

where they were going. She asked the constable many times. He wouldn't say.

Late in the day, they arrived in Boston. Dorcas was tired and sore. She was relieved when the constable finally took her down from the horse. He brought her inside a grim-looking building.

"What is this place?" she asked.

"Welcome to Boston prison," a man said, taking her by the hand.

He led her down to a dark cell. Dorcas began to cry. This place was as bad as the place in Salem. Maybe even worse.

But the horror had only begun.

Inside the cell, Dorcas saw several other women. One was her mother, Sarah Good. All the women were chained to the walls.

Before Dorcas could even protest, the prison guard chained her to a wall, too. Then he turned and walked off.

Little Dorcas began to scream.

Dorcas Good did not leave Boston prison for nine months. When at last she was released, the little girl with the bright face and wide eyes was gone. In her place was a bleak creature with a thin face, dull eyes, and an empty stare.

For the rest of her life, Dorcas Good had to be cared for by others.

Chapter 17

With Rebecca Nurse and Dorcas Good on their way to jail, the people of Salem Village felt some relief. Perhaps there was reason to be hopeful.

The villagers returned to the meetinghouse that same afternoon. Reverend Deodat Lawson, the minister visiting from Boston, was giving a sermon.

Reverend Lawson lost no time in getting to the point. What he had seen in Salem had alarmed him. He wanted the people to know exactly what they were up against, and what they had to do.

It was a long, stirring sermon. The minister used strong and frightening words to describe Satan's evil. He spoke of the Devil attacking people's bodies while going after their souls. He warned the villagers that their sins had brought evil and torment upon them.

Reverend Lawson urged the people to do everything they could to fight off the Devil. If they had to cry out against a friend or neighbor, then so be it. Satan's wicked work must be stopped. Even those persons who seem most devout may be instruments of the Devil, he told them. The people must remain ever on their guard.

"It is certain that Satan never works more like the Prince of Darkness than when he looks most like an angel of light," the minster declared.

Many people in the meetinghouse nodded in agreement. The minister's words were helping them understand how someone who appeared innocent, such as Rebecca Nurse or little Dorcas, could in fact be an agent of Satan.

Reverend Lawson finished his powerful sermon by urging the congregation to remain strong in their faith. Prayer is the antidote to the Devil's venom, he told them. "Pray! Pray!"

Chapter 18

Not everyone in Salem was convinced that Satan, and Satan alone, was the cause of all the trouble. Some people wondered if the afflicted girls' behavior was always genuine. Others thought that matters had gotten a little out of hand. Could Rebecca Nurse truly be a witch? It just didn't seem possible.

Most people kept their doubts to themselves, however. They did not want to go against the magistrates. They also feared the afflicted girls. After all, the girls could point their fingers at anyone. Look at Martha Corey. She had expressed doubt. Now she was in jail.

Still, some people did make their feelings known. Relatives and friends of Rebecca Nurse, for example, were collecting signatures in her support. Surprisingly, Sarah Holton signed the petition. She was the neighbor who had accused Rebecca of causing her husband's death.

One man who spoke his mind was John Proctor. Proctor was a successful farmer and businessman. His servant, Mary Warren, had been one of the afflicted girls at Rebecca Nurse's hearing. Proctor let it be known that he wished he hadn't let Mary go to the hearing. He said that before long the girls would be calling everyone in the village a witch.

Instead of listening to the girls' every word, Proctor offered people another suggestion. The girls should be whipped! In fact, when Mary Warren had first started acting strangely around the Proctor home, John Proctor threatened to beat her if she didn't get back to her chores. Mary did as told. Not until Proctor left the house did Mary again act "afflicted."

John Proctor showed courage in speaking out. But his words would soon prove costly.

Chapter 19

The Sunday after Reverend Lawson's memorable sermon, Reverend Parris gave a sermon of his own. Salem Village's minister chose his words carefully. He knew he had to address the villagers' concerns.

From the pulpit, Reverend Parris looked out over the people. His dark brown eyes slowly swept the room. His face was stern. Not even their sacred church, he began to explain, was wholly safe from Satan. Their congregation, like a garden, could have weeds among the flowers. Not just the best people, but also the worst, might be found in their church, the minister said. Indeed, some persons in their midst might prove to be as vile and wicked as the Devil himself.

Suddenly, a woman sprang up from her seat. She glared at the minister. Then she stormed out of the meetinghouse, slamming the door.

The room buzzed. Such behavior was shocking, especially during a Puritan church service.

"Who was that?" several people asked in a whisper.

"Sarah Cloyce," came the reply.

"Ah . . . small wonder, then."

Sarah Cloyce was one of Rebecca Nurse's two younger sisters. Reverend Parris' words were more than she could bear. Just three days earlier, Rebecca had been taken to jail. Now here was the minister implying that kindly, God-fearing Rebecca was not a saint, but a foul sinner.

Sarah was outraged. Where was the minister's charity? His mercy? How could he coldly turn on a woman who all her life had been faithful to the Lord in word and deed? And before she'd even had a trial! Sarah vowed never again to attend a church service led by the Reverend Samuel Parris.

But Sarah Cloyce soon had other concerns besides the minister. Within days of her stormy exit from the meetinghouse, the afflicted girls had a vision. They saw a group of witches standing in a field mocking church services by holding their own sort of Devil's service. As part of their ceremony, the witches ate red bread and drank blood.

And leading this strange service was a woman the girls recognized at once—Sarah Cloyce.

In the following days, the afflicted girls had more visions of Sarah Cloyce. Finally, on April 8, a warrant was issued for her arrest.

A second arrest warrant was also issued on April 8. This one was for Elizabeth Proctor, wife of John Proctor.

Ann Putnam had named Goody Proctor. Ann said that she had seen Goody Proctor's specter together with the specters of Tituba, Sarah Good, and Sarah Osborne. Goody Proctor had pinched and bitten her, Ann said. Later, Mercy Lewis claimed that she too had been tormented by Elizabeth Proctor. Other afflicted girls soon said much the same.

The hearings of Sarah Cloyce and Elizabeth Proctor were set for April 11. Unlike earlier hearings, these would not take place in Salem Village. Instead, they would be held in Salem Town. The meetinghouse there was larger. Salem Town was also a more convenient location for certain important people who would be there.

Talk of witchcraft was spreading beyond the village. What had begun as a local matter was drawing attention throughout the colony. People were afraid. The hunt for witches was gaining momentum.

Chapter 20

The Salem Town meetinghouse was crowded on the morning of April 11. Many people had traveled two or three hours from Salem Village to attend the hearings of Sarah Cloyce and Elizabeth Proctor. The rest of the seats were filled with people from Salem Town and the surrounding area.

In a way, these hearings were more significant than the earlier ones. Not only were they the first to take place outside Salem Village, but they were conducted by people of greater importance than John Hathorne and Jonathan Corwin.

Thomas Danforth himself ran the hearings. Danforth was deputy governor of the Massachusetts colony. His position was even higher than his title suggests. Governor Simon Bradstreet was almost ninety years old and in poor health. Thus, Danforth was, in effect, the person in charge of the colony.

Had Governor Bradstreet been in control rather than Danforth, events might have turned out differently. Bradstreet did not think the same way Danforth did. Unlike Danforth, Bradstreet would probably have doubted much of the testimony given at the hearings. He would not have been swayed by evidence based only on specters.

In fact, the very idea of "spectral evidence," as it was called, later became the main point of debate. Until that time, however, most people—including Hathorne, Danforth, and other judges—took spectral evidence as proof of guilt.

Spectral evidence was all but impossible to counter. What defense could anyone have against charges of witchcraft made against his or her specter? A woman could be asleep in bed while her spectral shape was supposedly hurting someone across town. If judges believed the afflicted person's testimony—which they almost always did—the accused witch was powerless to refute it. Even if other witnesses said they didn't see a specter, that made no difference. The judges believed the afflicted person. They felt certain that God had given the afflicted person eyes with which to see the Devil's agents.

Thus, an accusation alone became enough to "prove" someone guilty of witchcraft. The accuser's charges were believed. The accused's denials were not. For this reason, the afflicted girls had great power, and people were afraid to speak against them.

Thomas Danforth's attitude at the hearings of Cloyce and Proctor was much the same as that of John Hathorne at the earlier hearings. From the start, spectral evidence was proof enough of guilt.

The deputy governor was not the only high-ranking person at the Salem Town hearings. Six other colony officials also took part. Among them was Samuel Sewall, a Boston minister. Sewall was known to be a reasonable man. Yet, like Danforth and the others, he came to Salem expecting to find guilt, not innocence. John Hathorne, Jonathan Corwin, Reverend Samuel Parris, and Reverend Nicholas Noyes also attended the hearings. They, too, came looking for witches.

Danforth led the questioning. He asked the afflicted girls about the specters they had seen. The girls spoke of Goody Cloyce and Goody Proctor. Danforth asked who had tormented them. Again they named Goody Cloyce and Goody Proctor.

Abigail Williams and Mary Walcott added that they had seen a group of forty witches eating and drinking together. Sarah Cloyce and Sarah Good led them. Also part of the group were Sarah's sister, Rebecca Nurse, and Martha Corey.

Danforth listened closely. He rarely seemed surprised by what the girls said. Perhaps he knew in advance what their answers would be. Perhaps he was simply hearing what he had expected to hear.

Joining the afflicted girls was a new witness: the slave John Indian, Tituba's husband. Since his wife's confession, John had claimed that he too was afflicted. Maybe he made the claim only because he feared being accused himself. In any case, he came forward to testify against Sarah Cloyce.

Sarah glared at him.

"When did I ever hurt you?" she demanded.

"Many times," John Indian answered. He described how both Goody Cloyce and Goody Proctor had choked and pinched him. "They wanted me to put my mark in the Devil's book, sir," he told Danforth.

Sarah exploded in anger. "You are a liar!" she shouted.

Her outburst did no good. The afflicted girls went into fits. John Indian joined them. So did Goody Pope and Goody Bibber. Several girls screamed that a yellow bird—Sarah's familiar— was flying around her head.

Sarah Cloyce sank back in her chair. She felt weak. She shook her head, as much in despair as in horror.

Danforth ordered Sarah Cloyce held for trial. Sarah was taken away. She would join her sister in jail.

After Sarah Cloyce, Danforth and the others turned their attention to Elizabeth Proctor. Like Rebecca Nurse, Elizabeth had a kind and gentle nature. Unlike her husband, who sometimes lost his temper, Elizabeth seldom raised her voice in anger.

Danforth asked the afflicted girls if Goody Proctor had hurt them. At first, they all kept silent. Even Abigail Williams, Ann Putnam, and Mercy Lewis said nothing. Perhaps they did not speak because they had been bewitched into silence. Maybe they hesitated because they knew many people doubted that Elizabeth Proctor could be a witch.

Danforth turned to John Indian. "Has this woman hurt you?" he asked.

John glanced at Elizabeth Proctor, then nodded.

"She came to me and choked me."

"Did she bring the book with her?"

"Yes, sir. She wanted me to write in it."

Danforth looked at Elizabeth. "What do you say to this?"

"God is my witness that I know nothing of this," she said softly. Her eyes went to her husband, who was seated with the crowd. John Proctor's face was grim, his fists clenched. He wanted to jump up and yell, "Lies! All lies!" But he forced himself to stay seated and quiet.

Danforth turned again to the afflicted girls. Once more, he asked whether Goody Proctor had hurt them. This time they did not remain silent. They agreed with John Indian. Yes, they said. Goody Proctor had hurt them, too.

Hearing this, Elizabeth Proctor stared at the afflicted girls. What would make these children say such a thing about her? she wondered. Elizabeth loved children and would never hurt one. She herself was a mother of five. In fact, she was expecting a sixth child.

Under Elizabeth's steady gaze, the girls began having fits. They screamed and moaned and fell to the floor, as they had done so often before.

Danforth waited for them to quiet down.

"Did Goody Proctor bring the Devil's book with her when she came to you?" he asked the girls.

"Yes," they all said.

"She even boasted that she'd had her servant Mary Warren sign it," Abigail Williams added. Since the Proctors had kept Mary home, she was not there to comment on this.

Elizabeth looked at Abigail sadly.

"Dear child," she said, "it is not so. There is another judgment, dear child." Elizabeth wanted to remind Abigail that someday she would have to answer to God for what she said and did.

Abigail's response was to have another fit. Ann Putnam immediately joined her, followed by the others.

Suddenly, Abigail pointed to a wooden beam overhead.

"Look," she yelled. "There sits Goody Proctor's shape upon the beam!"

"Yes, I see it," cried Ann Putnam instantly.

"Yes, yes," shouted the others.

People screamed. Those seated beneath the beam scattered in every direction.

This was too much for John Proctor. He could keep quiet no longer. He leaped to his feet, roaring in protest. A good whipping was what these girls needed, he yelled. A good whipping would cure them of their visions. Or, better yet, hang them!

The girls reacted at once. Abigail Williams and Ann Putnam cried out that John Proctor was pinching them. They accused him of being a wizard, a male witch.

Proctor shouted back that they were liars. Then all the afflicted girls began screaming and moaning and having fits. Their awful cries filled the meetinghouse.

"Look!" Abigail yelled above all the noise. "Goodman Proctor's shape goes to Goody Pope!"

Instantly, Goody Pope shrieked and fell to the floor.

"Now he goes to Goody Bibber!" Ann Putnam screamed.

Goody Bibber had a terrible fit.

The meetinghouse was in an uproar. People were shouting, crying, running about. Several people fainted. Others ran out the door. The afflicted girls were howling and twisting. John Proctor was yelling and shaking his fist and demanding a stop to all the foolishness.

When it was finally over, when order had at last been restored, two more accused persons were on their way to jail. Elizabeth and John Proctor would both stand trial for witchcraft.

Chapter 21

Abigail Williams' statement that Mary Warren had signed the Devil's book did not pass unnoticed. In fact, soon after Elizabeth Proctor's hearing, Mary was arrested. Charges had been brought against her by the afflicted girls. At Rebecca Nurse's hearing, Mary had been one of these girls. Now the same girls charged her with witchcraft.

On April 19, Mary faced John Hathorne and Jonathan Corwin in the Salem Village meetinghouse. Hathorne posed the question that Mary was asking herself.

"Not long ago you were an afflicted person," the magistrate said. "Now you are an afflicter. How has this come to pass?"

Mary felt more alone than she ever had in her life. Her master and mistress, the Proctors, had both been taken to jail. The two magistrates were glaring at her, as was Reverend Parris. The crowd was whispering and pointing at her. And worst of all, the girls she thought of as her friends were calling her a witch.

How quickly the tables had turned. It was her own fault, Mary knew. From the start, she'd had some doubts. All the rumors and stories about witches and the Devil scared her. But they confused her, too. Nevertheless, like the other girls, Mary had quickly gotten swept up in events.

In the days after Rebecca Nurse's hearing, Mary had second thoughts. What was real, and what wasn't? Sometimes Mary wasn't sure anymore. Was she truly afflicted? Or, had she just been carried along by the emotional tide of the other girls?

When her mistress and master were accused, Mary felt more troubled than ever. She could not believe that the Proctors were witches.

John Proctor was a good man, a fair man. True, he did have a temper. He had threatened her with terrible punishment if she didn't stop babbling about witchcraft and return to work. At times he had even struck her. But that didn't make him a wizard.

And Goody Proctor? Mary had rarely heard her mistress speak a mean word. Could she be a witch?

Yet, Abigail and Ann and the other girls had all agreed that the Proctors had hurt them. They had screamed and choked and rolled about on the floor, just as at Goody Nurse's hearing.

Surely her friends couldn't be pretending, could they? More likely the girls' minds were just playing tricks on them just as her own mind must have played tricks on her.

Mary had voiced this very thought. And that's when her own troubles began.

Mary told several people that she had been mistaken. She should not have joined the afflicted girls in their testimony and in their fits. Indeed, Mary said, the afflicted girls must all have been mistaken. The specters they see are products of the imagination. Some kind of hallucinations. Not true evidence at all.

It was not long before the other girls found out what Mary was saying. They reacted as they usually did when someone doubted them—they began having fits. And they turned on Mary Warren, accusing her of witchcraft.

The logic was clear. The Devil must be using Mary. He saw how well the afflicted girls had been ridding Salem of witches. He wanted to stop them. How better to do this than to use one of the afflicted girls herself.

Mary heard the charges against her, and her stomach dropped. Standing before the magistrates, she was terrified. The afflicted girls stared at her. Several of them began having fits. They named Mary as the cause.

"I look up to God," Mary said, when Hathorne asked her to explain her change of heart. "I take it to be a great mercy of God."

Hathorne's face was like stone. "You take it to be a great mercy to afflict others?"

Before Mary could reply, the afflicted girls' crying and moaning grew louder. Several girls fell to the floor. Their bodies jerked and twisted. Their limbs stiffened. They made choking sounds.

Panic gripped Mary. She felt utterly alone, utterly defenseless. Her mind raced. She didn't know what to do or what to say. Was all this witchery real, or was it only in the girls' minds? Could she truly be causing the horrible fits she was seeing? Was Satan behind all of this?

The girls' cries were terrible. Mary couldn't stand to hear them. Suddenly, she herself began to shake. Tears streamed down her cheeks. She heard herself sobbing and couldn't stop. She struggled to speak. But her jaws locked, and she couldn't get a word out.

One of the afflicted girls yelled that Goodman Proctor and his wife were keeping Mary from speaking. Another girl saw the specter of Martha Corey.

Mary stood there helplessly. She couldn't think straight. She couldn't think at all.

"I am sorry," she wept. "I am sorry."

The afflicted girls wailed even more loudly. All of them were having fits now.

Mary sank to her knees. Her face was wet with tears. Her whole body was shaking and twitching.

"Lord help me!" she pleaded. "Lord save me!" She sprawled on the floor. "I will tell . . ." Her body jerked and twisted. "They brought me to it!" She was crying hard now. Then she began to choke and shudder. Before long, she was having fits as violent as those of the other girls.

Hathorne waited. But every time Mary started to recover, another fit came on. Finally, the magistrate ordered Mary to be carried out of the meetinghouse. Several other accused witches were to be questioned that day. Hathorne had no more time to waste.

The magistrates continued to examine Mary for the next three weeks. Some days they questioned her at the meetinghouse. Other days they came to her jail cell.

At first, Mary tried to insist that she really had been mistaken. But the magistrates did not believe her. Neither did Reverend Parris, who also questioned her at times. Everyone believed that Mary was under the influence of witches— or that she herself was a witch.

Day after day the men fired the same questions at her. Mary cried and pleaded. But no one would accept her answers.

After the men left, Mary huddled in her dim and dirty jail cell. Her stomach growled. Like other prisoners, she got little to eat or drink.

At last, she could stand it no longer. Mary

stopped trying to explain herself. She confessed that she had been bewitched. She named first Elizabeth Proctor, then John Proctor, as witches.

Under questioning, she also accused several other persons of witchcraft.

The magistrates were satisfied. They released Mary from jail. She rejoined the afflicted girls. Her friends seemed pleased to have her return.

Never again did Mary Warren express any doubts.

Chapter 22

One of the accused waiting to be questioned after Mary Warren on April 19 was Giles Corey. Giles was Martha Corey's eighty-year-old husband. He was a grouchy, stubborn man. He and his wife often argued.

During Martha's hearing, Giles had made complaints about his wife. These added to the suspicions about her. But now it was Giles' turn to face the magistrates. He, too, had been charged with witchcraft. His accusers were Ann Putnam, Mercy Lewis, Abigail Williams, Mary Walcott, and Elizabeth Hubbard.

Giles Corey fared no better than Martha Corey had. Hathorne did not like the old man's answers or his attitude. When Giles denied saying things that witnesses had heard him say, he sealed his fate. The Puritans took lying very seriously. Hathorne's decision was made. He ordered Giles taken to jail.

The next person called before the magistrates was Bridget Bishop. No one in Salem was surprised to see this woman brought into the meetinghouse.

There had been dark rumors about Bridget Bishop for years. Long before the events of 1692, people had suspected that Bridget was a witch. And, in her case, they had some cause.

Bridget's first husband had died under suspicious circumstances. It was whispered that he had been bewitched by his wife. Later, in 1680, charges of witchcraft were again made against Bridget. She was even brought to trial, though not convicted. More recently, her present husband had been heard to say that his wife "was familiar with the Devil," and that "she sat up all the night long" with him.

People spread many tales about Bridget Bishop. They said that she worked black magic through charms and spells. One story described how she had bewitched a horse. Another told how she caused a farmer's cart to break.

Several people claimed to have been visited by Bridget's specter. They knew at once it was Bridget Bishop. They recognized the flashy, brightly colored clothes she liked to wear.

Some rumors were far more serious. It was said that Bridget had used witchcraft to harm her enemies—even to kill several children.

Hathorne had heard the stories about Bridget. He knew that many people feared her.

There was no sympathy in his voice when he spoke to her.

"These girls accuse you of hurting them," the magistrate said. He gestured toward Abigail Williams, Ann Putnam, Mercy Lewis, Mary Walcott, and Elizabeth Hubbard. "What do you say to this?"

Bridget frowned. She looked at the five afflicted girls who had come to the meetinghouse today. But Bridget lived in Salem Town, not Salem Village. She did not know any of them.

"I have never seen these persons," she said.

Hathorne asked his usual questions. Bridget denied the charges. The magistrate then asked about some of the rumors he'd heard about her. Bridget insisted that she was innocent.

Hathorne asked more questions. As Bridget answered, the five afflicted girls began to imitate her movements. Sometimes they screamed in pain as they moved. Bridget bent forward; the girls bent forward. She shook her head; the girls shook their heads. She raised her eyes; the girls raised their eyes.

Hathorne had seen such witchery before, at the hearings of Martha Corey, Rebecca Nurse, and others. Bridget, however, did not know what to make of this display.

"You still say that you are not a witch?" Hathorne said.

"No, sir, I am not. I know nothing of this. I don't know what a witch is."

Hathorne leaned toward her. "If you don't know what a witch is, how can you be certain that you are not one?"

Bridget looked at him blankly. She didn't know how to answer.

"I am innocent," was all she could manage.

Hathorne did not believe her. Neither did anyone else. Bridget Bishop was taken to jail.

Chapter 23

The hunt for witches had started slowly. But it was gaining speed at a frightening rate.

At first, only one or two arrest warrants had been written at a time. Now warrants were being issued in batches. By the end of April, nearly thirty people had been charged with witchcraft. That number would more than double by late May.

It appeared that anyone could be accused: young or old, good reputation or bad, village resident or not. Even the richest shipowner in Salem, Philip English, was charged.

Of all those accused, the magistrates released just *one* person: a man named Nehemiah Abbott. His was the only case in which the afflicted girls disagreed. Ann Putnam told Hathorne that Abbott's specter had hurt them. But Mercy Lewis said that Goodman Abbott was not the right man. The other girls were not sure. Finally, Hathorne allowed Abbott to go.

No one else was as lucky as Abbott. Indeed, many people were decidedly *un*lucky. They saw their family members or relatives accused right along with them. For example, both of Rebecca Nurse's sisters were jailed: first Sarah Cloyce, and then, less than two weeks later, Rebecca's other sister Mary Easty. Often, both wife and husband were sent to jail, as were Elizabeth and John Proctor and Martha and Giles Corey. Sometimes charges were filed against the parent or child of an accused witch, such as Sarah Good's daughter Dorcas.

Weeks of accusations and arrests only added to people's fears. In addition, as charges flew and jails filled, a new fear steadily grew.

At the start, people worried about individual witches—Tituba, Sarah Good, Sarah Osborne. But now there was increasing talk about *groups* of witches.

In early March, Tituba reported nine marks in the Devil's book. People wondered who else had signed the book. In the weeks since then, the afflicted girls had several times spoken of witches gathering to hold their own services. The idea of such an organized society of witches kept many a villager awake at night.

Then, in late April, a woman named Deliverance Hobbs was called before the magistrates. Her testimony disturbed the people even more.

Deliverance confessed to being a witch. A few days earlier, her daughter, Abigail, had done the same. Abigail Hobbs had been a wild-spirited child all her young life. Now in her twenties, Abigail did not hesitate to give all sorts of details about the Devil and his ways. In fact, she seemed to enjoy telling her stories to the magistrates.

Deliverance was less imaginative than her daughter. She was also much more afraid. Under questioning, she mostly agreed with whatever was suggested to her.

Meanwhile, William Hobbs—Deliverance's husband and Abigail's father—kept insisting that he had nothing to do with witchcraft. His denials did him no good. In the end, William followed Abigail and Deliverance to jail.

Deliverance's testimony sent new chills through Salem. She described a large group of witches assembling in the field near Reverend Parris' house. There they held their mocking Devil's services, drinking red wine and eating red bread.

Deliverance named several witches who had been present at these services, including Rebecca Nurse. She also said that a preacher led the services. This preacher instructed the witches to bewitch every man, woman, and child in Salem Village.

People shuddered when they heard this. Who could this evil person be? Who was leading this company of witches in its attack on Salem?

When Deliverance named the preacher, people gasped. The leader of the witches was a man whom many of them knew. He was a *minister.* In fact, ten years before, he had been the minister of Salem Village! His name was George Burroughs.

Chapter 24

Many people were shocked to hear George Burroughs accused of witchcraft. Burroughs was a handsome, forty-year-old minister. He was a graduate of Harvard. He was poised and well-spoken. Although he had lived in Salem Village for three years, he had moved to Maine in 1683. He had not returned to the village since.

But Burroughs had made some enemies while living in Salem Village. Among them, was the powerful Putnam family. It was Thomas Putnam and his brother-in-law who filed charges against Burroughs. A warrant was issued on April 30. The minister was arrested in Maine. On May 4, a constable brought George Burroughs back to Salem.

Burroughs' *specter,* however, had come to Salem some time before. At least, so said Ann Putnam and several of the other afflicted girls.

Shortly after Deliverance Hobbs named the minister, Ann Putnam had a series of awful visions. First, George Burroughs came to her and choked her, Ann said. He told her that he had made many people witches, including Abigail Hobbs. He tried to force Ann to sign the Devil's book. She refused. Then Burroughs told her that he had used witchcraft to kill many people, including children. He had also killed his first two wives.

Burroughs' specter returned to Ann some days later. This time he told her that the specters of his wives would appear to her. They will tell you lies, he warned. Don't listen.

Ann reported that the specters did indeed come, just as the minister said. This vision was the most horrifying of all. The two women appeared to Ann wearing the shrouds in which they had been buried. Then Burroughs appeared. The women turned toward him. Their pale faces became red and angry. You were cruel to us, they told him. You should pay for your cruelty. You should be cast into hell. At that, Burroughs disappeared.

Then the two specters turned to Ann. The color had left their faces again. They were as white as blank paper. The minister murdered us, they told Ann. One of them pulled aside her shroud to show Ann the wound that Burroughs had given her.

In later years, people would often discuss Ann's visions. The girl had been just two years old when Burroughs left Salem. She was only twelve now. Ann probably had never even met the minister. Yet, her visions included numerous details about Burroughs and his wives.

Had Thomas Putnam deliberately given his daughter the information? Had Ann simply overheard her family talking about Burroughs over the years? How much did Ann truly "see"? How much was the product of her imagination? How much was hallucination? As with so many of the accounts of specters and witchcraft, such questions have no clear answers. What *is* clear, however, is that in 1692, the people of Salem took Ann's words very seriously.

In addition, Ann was not the only one to report visions of George Burroughs. Elizabeth Hubbard, Mary Walcott, Mercy Lewis, and some of the other afflicted girls saw him, too. Several said that the minister had hurt them, as he had hurt Ann. He had also tried to get them to sign the Devil's book. Abigail Williams and Mary Warren, like Deliverance Hobbs, identified Burroughs as the leader of the witches. The weight of so much "evidence" was heavy indeed.

On May 9, George Burroughs faced not two, but four magistrates. Besides Hathorne and Corwin, Samuel Sewall and William Stoughton were present.

William Stoughton was a minister, too, as well as a government official. Later in May, Stoughton would succeed Thomas Danforth as deputy governor of the Massachusetts colony. Stoughton would also play a key role in the witch trials. He served as chief judge of the court.

Even in Maine, Burroughs had heard stories about events in Salem Village. But the minister was not prepared for the shock of meeting the afflicted girls face-to-face.

At first, Stoughton and the others questioned him alone. They asked about his life in Maine, his family, and his religious practices. They also asked about his first two wives, both of whom had died. Then Stoughton ordered the afflicted girls to come in. He instructed Burroughs to keep his eyes turned away from them. This would be a test.

The girls walked in and stood quietly off to one side. After a moment, Stoughton directed Burroughs to look at them. As soon as the minister did as told, most of the girls shrieked and fell to the floor. They rolled around, moaning and screaming. Several girls cried that the minister was biting them.

Burroughs stared at them in disbelief.

"What do you think of this?" Stoughton asked.

Burroughs shook his head. "I am amazed," he said. "I do not understand any of it."

Suddenly, one of the girls still on her feet cried out. She was eighteen-year-old Susannah Sheldon. Susannah shouted that ghosts of the minister's two dead wives were standing right there in front of her. Both were accusing Burroughs of murder.

Ann Putnam screamed and said, yes, she could see them, too.

The minister turned pale. But before he could speak, Susannah also collapsed to the floor. She began having a terrible fit. A moment later, several more girls started having fits. Stoughton ordered the afflicted girls removed from the room.

Next, the magistrates called villagers to give testimony. One after another they were brought in. Men and women, young and old. Some of the afflicted girls returned to repeat their stories.

With a sinking heart, Burroughs listened to the testimony. Each statement was stranger than the one before.

"He was standing in the field. Witches were all around him. Rebecca Nurse and John Proctor were there, too."

"He put the evil eye on me."

"I saw the Devil's book in his library."

"With just a finger or two, he can raise molasses barrels and hunting guns over his head. Only the Devil could grant a man such strength."

"He can read people's thoughts."

"He carried me to a mountaintop and promised me things, if I would sign the book."

More than twenty villagers spoke in all. Burroughs denied all their charges. But his words were no match for specters and visions.

"Take him to the jail," Stoughton ordered.

Chapter 25

By late May, more than seventy suspected witches were in jail. The afflicted girls were naming not just people they knew. They were also naming people they had never met. The accused lived not only in Salem Village or Salem Town. Many lived in Topsfield, Beverly, Reading, and other towns.

How could the afflicted girls name strangers? This was a troubling question. Often, the girls explained that the specters identified themselves. This answer did not satisfy everyone. It was more likely that the girls knew some of the accused by reputation. In other instances, Thomas Putnam or someone else may have suggested names to the girls. Sometimes the girls simply confirmed charges made by someone else.

The magistrates should have given this issue more thought. But they were intent upon finding witches. They were battling with the Devil. They had to win. They looked to the afflicted girls— God's witnesses—to help them.

This eagerness to defeat Satan led the magistrates to believe whatever the girls said. It also made them ignore certain details they should have questioned. The girls' hysterical fits made their testimony all the more convincing. Time and again, the magistrates took the girls' words as proof of guilt.

The case of John Alden was one such instance. Alden was a well-known and highly respected Boston sea captain. On May 28, he was accused of witchcraft along with ten other people.

Alden was outraged at the charges. He did not know the afflicted girls, and they did not know him. Yet, because of these girls, the deputy governor had ordered him to come to Salem Village.

At the hearing on May 31, the afflicted girls did not at first identify Alden. He was one of many people in the room whom the girls had never met. Nevertheless, the girls stared into the faces around them. Then they fell to the floor, crying and moaning.

"Who is hurting you?" John Hathorne asked. He was one of three magistrates that day. The other two were Jonathan Corwin and a Salem man named Bartholomew Gedney. Gedney had known Alden for many years. In fact, the two men had been to sea together.

The girls kept on wailing, but named no one.

"Who is hurting you?" Hathorne repeated.

Still the girls named no one.

Then a man whom Alden did not know came up behind one of the afflicted girls. He helped her to her feet. As she rose, the man whispered something in her ear.

A moment later, the girl cried out, "*Alden*. It is *Alden* who is hurting me."

Before long, all the afflicted girls agreed. They all named Alden as the one hurting them.

"Confess!" Bartholomew Gedney urged Alden. Gedney had always thought highly of the sea captain. But the afflicted girls had changed his mind.

Alden was furious. Who were these lunatic girls? How dare they accuse him? Were they playing tricks? Or were they all just mad? Or maybe it was they who were possessed by the Devil!

Alden told Gedney and the others that he had nothing to confess to. He was innocent.

"Why would I come to Salem Village to hurt people I don't even know?" he asked. Then he looked angrily at the afflicted girls.

Instantly, they began having fits again.

Alden was not impressed. He looked hard at Gedney.

"Why is it that *you* don't fall down when I look at *you*?" he demanded.

Gedney did not answer. Instead, the magistrates called for the "touch test."

The touch test was an often used way of proving an accused witch's guilt. The test was based on the belief that a witch's evil power could be turned back if the victim and the witch touched. The evil would flow from the victim back into the witch. The afflicted person would then be well.

One by one, the afflicted girls were brought over to Alden. Alden was told to turn his head away. If he looked at any of the girls, he might make them worse instead of better.

Alden's hand was guided to touch the hand of each girl, one at a time. Each girl in turn appeared to recover.

The magistrates nodded. The man's guilt was clear.

Alden shook his head in disgust.

"How can God allow these creatures to accuse innocent people?" he demanded. "They speak not a word of truth."

But the magistrates were convinced. They ordered Alden to prison.

Fortunately for John Alden, he had many friends. In September, they helped him escape. Eventually, the captain's name was cleared.

Others were not so fortunate. Sarah Osborne, one of the first to be accused of witchcraft, had been in prison since March. In May, about two weeks before John Alden's arrest, Sarah died.

Chapter 26

It was not surprising that a sickly older woman like Sarah Osborne died in prison. The prisons in which the accused witches waited for trial were horrible places. They were dirty, dark, and damp. They smelled of unwashed bodies and human waste. In winter, they were freezing cold.

Prisoners received little food or water. Usually there were several prisoners in a cell. But as the witch hunt went on, jails became more crowded.

Witches—the most dangerous prisoners—were chained to the walls. Oddly enough, people believed that chaining witches kept their specters from hurting anyone. This belief gained support whenever a witch's specter stopped appearing after the witch was put in jail.

Accused witches were viewed as agents of the Devil. As such, they often suffered cruel treatment. They had to endure hour after hour of harsh questioning. Jailers, ministers, and others came to their cells to try to get them to confess. Sometimes accused witches were forced to remain standing for endless hours. Sometimes they were kept awake all night. They were watched to see if a familiar came to visit them.

In addition, their whole bodies were searched, inch by inch, for "witch's marks." These were places from where a familiar was thought to suck blood. Searchers commonly stuck pins or needles into suspected witch's marks. Such "pricking" was a test. A witch's mark supposedly had no feeling and would not bleed when stuck.

Some accused witches were tortured to force them to confess. One method of torture was to "tie neck and heels." The prisoner's neck was tied to her feet, sometimes for a day or more.

The hardships were more than physical. The accused witches had left behind family members, young and old. Who would care for the babies? The children? The old people? Prisoners also worried about their farms and homes. Who would tend the crops? Who would attend to the livestock? What if the sheriff seized their property, as often happened?

To make matters even worse, all prisoners had to pay for their imprisonment. Whether or not they were found guilty did not matter. They had to pay for room and board, clothing, legal fees—even for their chains! Many of the accused witches had little money to begin with. Prison costs were more than they could afford.

The horrors of prison caused many accused witches to wish for a speedy trial. Either they would be found innocent and released, or they would be found guilty and hanged. Either way, they would at last be free.

However, even though it was May, and the jails were rapidly filling, not one trial had yet been held. The Massachusetts colony still had not received its new charter from England. Without it, only hearings, not trials, could take place.

The accused witches had no choice but to wait, hope, and pray.

Chapter 27

In mid-May, the new charter finally arrived by ship from England. Aboard the same ship was the newly appointed governor, Sir William Phips.

After his long journey, the new governor was surprised to find the colony in an uproar. Everywhere, there was talk of witches and specters. The stories the governor heard were strange and alarming. And even though witches already filled the jails, arrests were continuing.

Governor Phips knew that he had to act quickly. He had to do what was necessary to protect the people against this attack by the Devil. Phips also knew that accused criminals should not be kept in jail for weeks or months without a trial. Furthermore, witchcraft was a most serious crime. Once tried and convicted, witches were to be put to death. It was the law.

Within two weeks, Governor Phips established a special court. It was called the Court of Oyer and Terminer ("to hear and determine"). This court would run the witchcraft trials. The chief judge would be William Stoughton, the new deputy governor. The other judges appointed were Samuel Sewall, Bartholomew Gedney, Nathaniel Saltonstall, Peter Sergent, John Richards, and Wait Winthrop. All these men were experienced and well-known magistrates.

The witchcraft trials would be held in Salem Town. While the trials went on, hearings for other suspected witches would also continue.

A jury of twelve male church members would be chosen to decide the guilt or innocence of the accused. Just as at the hearings, no lawyers would take part in the trials. The Puritans held a low opinion of lawyers. They did not allow them to practice law in the colony. Judge Stoughton followed the Puritans' policy.

Word of the special court came as welcome news. In less than three months, about 150 accused witches had been jailed. These witches and their specters had afflicted many people. Prayer and fasting—the Puritans' usual defense against Satan—had done little good. Hanging the witches was the only sure way to stop them and their Devil's work.

Many people welcomed the special court for another reason. They could not stand seeing their relatives and friends suffer in the miserable jails. They wanted them put on trial. Then the accused could show their innocence.

Indeed, the sight of respectable people in prison raised doubts among many people. Had the whole situation gotten out of hand? Could such people as Rebecca Nurse and both of her sisters, Sarah Cloyce and Mary Easty, truly be witches?

But if some voices expressed doubt, most did not. People remembered only too well the frightening hearings, the shocking testimony. And if anyone for a moment forgot, the afflicted girls were there to remind them. No, there was no room for doubt. The Devil and his agents were in Salem. And their evil was spreading!

Some of the accused persons confessed under the pressure of prison conditions. Some confessed after harsh treatment or torture. Some became convinced that they really *were* witches. Their hysteria resembled that of the afflicted girls. Other accused witches confessed in hopes of escaping the hangman's noose. Ironically, confessed witches were spared. Those who claimed innocence were not.

The first of the Salem witchcraft trials was set for June 2. The accused witch who was chosen to face the Court of Oyer and Terminer was the one with the most evidence against her: Bridget Bishop.

Bridget had been tried for witchcraft before, in 1680. That time, she had gone free. In 1692, she would not be so lucky.

Chapter 28

In Europe, during the sixteenth and seventeenth centuries, witches were hanged or burned by the thousands. Fortunately, witch hunting never reached that scale in America. Still, the fear of witches left its mark, especially in New England.

A small number of witchcraft trials had taken place in New England before 1692. Typically, one neighbor accused another of causing harm or illness. Most of those accused were not convicted. Of those who were, only about fifteen were hanged in the fifty years before the Salem trials.

The Salem trials were much more significant than earlier New England trials. No previous outbreak of witchcraft had been as large or as frightening. And no outbreak had caused such widespread hysteria.

In Salem, accusers spoke not of a single witch casting an evil eye on a neighbor. They spoke of great numbers of witches coming together to threaten an entire population. The suspected witches included many respected members of the community—even a minister.

Some of the accused were charged with terrible crimes. For example, Goody Putnam accused Rebecca Nurse of murdering fourteen people. Most of those were children.

The Salem witch trials finally began in June 1692. The largest witch hunt ever to occur in America was about to enter its deadliest phase.

After six weeks in jail, Bridget Bishop was relieved to get out. Traveling from Boston prison to Salem Town was better than being chained in a dark cell.

Her relief, though, was short-lived. On her way to court, Bridget glanced at the Salem meetinghouse. At that moment, there was a loud crash inside the building. Several people ran inside to see what happened. They found that a heavy wooden board had fallen.

"She must have sent a demon inside to pull it loose," someone said.

Others agreed. The constables guarding Bridget later reported the event. At Bridget's trial, this incident became more proof that she was a witch. It was well known that a witch's evil eye could harm person or property.

Entering the courthouse, Bridget thought

back to her hearing in Salem Village. She remembered the five girls who had accused her, girls she didn't even know. Everyone at the hearing had believed them. No one had believed her. Bridget hoped that her trial would be different.

But Bridget Bishop was the first of the accused witches to learn an awful truth. Her earlier hearing counted heavily against her. In fact, in the eyes of the Court of Oyer and Terminer, her guilt had been all but proved. The testimony given in court only confirmed what the judges and jury already believed.

Whatever hope Bridget had soon faded. Before her trial, her body was carefully searched for witch's marks. Such a mark was indeed found.

First, the falling wooden board. Now, the witch's mark. Bridget knew that things were starting off badly. They would only get worse.

In the courtroom, the afflicted girls took one look at Bridget and started having fits. Bridget's specter was biting, choking, and pinching them, the girls cried.

Bridget tried to protest her innocence. But whenever she looked toward the afflicted girls, they screamed and fell to the floor. At times, they imitated her movements, just as they had done at her hearing.

Bridget looked at William Stoughton and the other judges. She looked at the jurors. Everyone's face was hard and cold. Bridget didn't know what to do or say. The cries of the afflicted girls rang in her ears.

The judges called for the touch test. Bridget was made to touch each afflicted girl. As soon as she did, the girl recovered. Everyone believed that Bridget's evil power was flowing from her victims back to her.

Witnesses were called to testify. Events that had happened at Bridget's hearing were reviewed. The evidence against her mounted.

Many townspeople spoke. They accused Bridget—or her specter—of all sorts of witchery. A man said that Bridget had bewitched his young son. A woman said that she had seen Bridget's specter taking part in Devil's services. Many stories first told at Bridget's hearing were repeated at the trial.

Then two workmen came forward to testify. Bridget had hired them to take down an old wall in a house where she lived. The workmen said that inside the wall they found several small dolls. The dolls had pins sticking in them. Bridget could not explain the workmen's discovery.

The courtroom buzzed. This was certain proof of witchcraft. Witches used dolls to work their evil magic. By hurting a doll that resembled a real person, a witch could harm that person.

Several members of the jury nodded. The judges appeared satisfied. The evidence was overwhelming. The afflicted girls' fits. The touch test. The townspeople's testimony. Attacks by Bridget's specter. Her evil eye. Her witch's mark. Her use of dolls to work black magic.

Bridget insisted that she was not a witch. No one paid attention.

The jurors had no trouble reaching a verdict. They found Bridget Bishop guilty. She was convicted of witchcraft against Abigail Williams, Ann Putnam, Mercy Lewis, Mary Walcott, and Elizabeth Hubbard.

The judges sentenced her to death by hanging.

Chapter 29

Early on the morning of June 10, Bridget Bishop was taken out of her jail cell. Still in chains, she was led outside to a waiting cart.

A crowd of people had gathered, children as well as adults. Hangings were public events. They served as a warning to would-be lawbreakers. Besides, Puritan parents wanted their children to see what happens to sinners.

The cart carried Bridget through the streets of Salem to a high, rocky hill at the western edge of town. This hill became known as Gallows Hill. Some called it Witches' Hill.

The crowd walked alongside and behind the cart. People shouted at Bridget. They mocked her. "Die, you witch!" someone called. "Now you'll get what you deserve!" cried someone else.

Slowly, the cart rumbled up the steep slope. It stopped close to the top of the hill, near an oak tree. Bridget was taken from the cart.

As the crowd watched, Bridget Bishop was hanged from a thick branch of the tree. When she was dead, her body was cut down. It was buried in the rocks on one side of the hill. No one said a prayer over her rocky grave.

Bridget Bishop was the first of the accused Salem witches to be executed. She would not be the last.

Chapter 30

Most of Salem's people felt that justice had been well served by hanging Bridget Bishop. Some, however, were not so sure.

Certainly the woman had earned more than her share of suspicion. But had there truly been enough evidence to convict and hang her?

Spectral evidence was the main issue. Could the Devil take the shape of an innocent person? If so, then a specter's evil deeds could not be used as proof of someone's guilt. Not Bridget's, or anyone else's.

However, most people believed that the Devil could take someone's shape only if that person agreed. Therefore, the person *was* to blame for whatever his or her specter did. This was what John Hathorne and the other magistrates at the hearings believed. William Stoughton and almost all the other judges at the trials shared this view, too. Nathaniel Saltonstall was the only judge who felt troubled enough after Bridget Bishop's hanging to resign from the Court of Oyer and Terminer.

Saltonstall was not the only official who felt uneasy. After the hanging, Governor Phips himself wrote to a respected group of Boston ministers. He asked for their advice. They replied in a letter on June 15.

The letter offered a somewhat mixed message. On one hand, the ministers warned against spectral evidence. They also warned against using the touch test. Such evidence by itself was not reliable, they wrote. On the other hand, the ministers praised the judges for their work. Then they urged the court to continue going after the witches. Proceed quickly and forcefully, the ministers advised.

How to react to this letter was up to the judges. The ministers could only offer their opinion.

Stoughton and the other members of the special court discussed the matter. In the end, their views did not change. Except for Saltonstall, who resigned, the judges agreed to keep using the same methods they had been using. They would continue to accept both spectral evidence and the touch test in future trials.

Their first opportunity came two weeks later. The trials of five more accused witches began on June 29. Among the five were Sarah Good and Rebecca Nurse.

Chapter 31

Five women went on trial at the end of June. Sarah Good and Rebecca Nurse were from Salem Village. Sarah Wilds and Elizabeth How were from Topsfield. Susannah Martin was from Amesbury.

None of the five had as much evidence against her as Bridget Bishop, but the afflicted girls were evidence enough. The testimony of witnesses called before the court added further proof. So did the touch test. Usually, though, it was spectral evidence and the girls' fits that doomed the accused witch.

Sometimes relatives and friends came forward. They spoke in defense of the accused. But such testimony could not stand against the screams of the afflicted. And when left to choose between testimony for and against a prisoner, the judges sided with the afflicted girls.

One telling example of the court's attitude

happened during Sarah Good's trial. One of the afflicted girls cried out that Sarah's specter had attacked her with a knife. The girl then showed the judges a piece of a blade. The piece had broken off from Sarah's knife, the girl said. Spectators nodded to one another. This was more proof of Sarah's witchcraft.

But one young man in the audience rose to his feet. He asked to address the court. William Stoughton, the chief judge, told him to speak.

The man said that he recognized the piece of blade. In fact, it had come from his own knife. He had broken the blade the day before, the man said. He remembered that the afflicted girl had been present at the time. The man then showed the judges his knife. The broken piece matched exactly.

Amazingly, Stoughton and the other judges had little reaction. They merely warned the girl to tell the truth. Then the trial went on as if nothing had happened. To no one's surprise, the jury found Sarah Good guilty of witchcraft. Sarah Wilds, Elizabeth How, and Susannah Martin were also found guilty. Their trials did not differ much from their hearings.

Of the five trials held at the end of June, Rebecca Nurse's trial drew the most attention.

Before the trial began, the elderly woman was searched for witch's marks. All the searchers except for one agreed that Rebecca had such a mark. Rebecca asked for a second search by different people. The court refused.

As Rebecca walked slowly into the courtroom, people whispered to one another. Many noted how awful she looked. Three months in prison had taken a heavy toll on the seventy-one-year-old woman. Her health had been poor before. Now, she was weaker than ever. Her face was thin and pale.

Rebecca's trial followed the same path as her hearing. The judges tried to maintain order. But at times this was all but impossible.

Goody Putnam, her daughter Ann, Abigail Williams, and the other afflicted girls accused Rebecca.

When Rebecca said that she was innocent of all the charges, the afflicted girls went into fits.

But Rebecca Nurse had many defenders. Some were relatives. Others were friends and neighbors. Many were themselves respected citizens.

One by one, Rebecca's supporters testified on her behalf. They told the court how deeply religious Rebecca was. They described what a kind and loving person she had always been. They swore that she was not guilty of the crimes of which she was accused. They presented petitions in her defense containing dozens of signatures. One of Rebecca's daughters even testified that she had seen an afflicted girl stick herself with pins and then accuse Rebecca of hurting her.

The jury was moved by all that they heard. They found it hard to believe Goody Putnam's claim that this gentle, soft-spoken old woman could bewitch children to death.

When Stoughton asked for their verdict, the foreman spoke up.

"Not guilty," he said.

There was a moment of surprised silence in the courthouse. Then pandemonium broke out.

The accused girls began to shriek and howl madly. They dropped to the floor, their bodies twisting. They rolled about, choking and crying. Their arms and legs flew in every direction. Their hysteria swept through the courtroom like a storm. Even some people in the audience started screaming.

The judges and jurors were all stunned. Most had seen the girls have fits before. But never had they heard or seen bedlam as wild as this.

Some of the judges expressed strong doubts about the verdict. Stoughton spoke to the jurors. He suggested that maybe they should give the matter more thought.

The jury did as told. They reconsidered everything that they had witnessed.

Then, once again, Stoughton asked for their verdict. This time the foreman had a different answer.

"Guilty," he said.

With that, Rebecca Nurse was sentenced to hang. So were Sarah Good, Sarah Wilds, Elizabeth How, and Susannah Martin.

Soon after Rebecca's death sentence, Reverend Nicholas Noyes pronounced another, equally harsh sentence. He had Rebecca excommunicated, or expelled, from the church.

For a woman as religious as Rebecca, this was the cruelest blow. Being excommunicated meant that she was damned to hell.

The excommunication ceremony took place in public. Rebecca was brought from prison to the Salem Town meetinghouse. She had to be helped inside, because she was too weak to walk.

Before a silent crowd, Reverend Noyes read the order. Rebecca, partially deaf, could not hear much of what was said. But she understood only too well what was happening. When it was over, Rebecca was taken back to prison. There she was chained to the wall, like all dangerous witches.

Rebecca Nurse's relatives and friends were outraged by her treatment. They brought a petition to Governor Phips. They made the strongest possible appeal on her behalf.

The governor considered the petition. He reviewed the events of the trial. He listened to the emotional pleas of Rebecca's family. Finally, he agreed to give Rebecca a reprieve.

But even this small victory did Rebecca no good.

Word soon spread that Rebecca Nurse had

been granted a reprieve. Immediately, the afflicted girls went into fits. They accused Rebecca of attacking them again.

To many people, this was fresh evidence of Rebecca's guilt. The girls' fits had stopped when Rebecca was taken to jail. Now that she was about to be set free, the girls were again under attack.

Several high-ranking people protested to the governor. They told him that he should not have granted Rebecca a reprieve. They reminded him that the woman was a convicted witch. They repeated all the evidence against her. They said that they feared for the lives of the afflicted girls if Rebecca Nurse continued to hurt them.

Governor Phips agreed that he had made a mistake. He canceled Rebecca's reprieve.

July 19 was set as the date for Rebecca Nurse's hanging. Sarah Good, Sarah Wilds, Elizabeth How, and Susannah Martin were all sentenced to hang with her.

Chapter 32

While the first trials were held, the arrests and hearings continued. Some of the accused were from Charlestown and Billerica. Others were from Andover and Lynn. Witches seemed to be living in towns across New England!

The pace of arrests had slowed during the first weeks after Bridget Bishop's hanging. But then accusations began to increase. More and more people were arrested and sent to jail. In fact, so many people were accused over the summer that officials could not keep accurate records.

On July 19, five convicted witches followed Bridget Bishop's route through Salem to Gallows Hill. Sarah Good, Rebecca Nurse, Sarah Wilds, Elizabeth How, and Susannah Martin rode the rumbling cart up the steep hill.

A large crowd walked alongside and behind the cart. The afflicted girls were there. So were many of the people who had spoken out against the prisoners in court.

The crowd jeered at the witches. Adults shouted insults and curses. Children called them names.

The five women, all in chains, looked grim. Some were standing. Others sat on the floor of the cart. Two were weeping. Sarah Good scowled and muttered. Rebecca Nurse closed her eyes in prayer.

The cart stopped near the top of Gallows Hill. The oak tree cast its large shadow across the hill. As the five women were taken from the cart, they eyed the tree with dread.

A ladder leaned against one thick branch of the oak. From this branch hung five nooses.

An executioner took the first prisoner up the ladder. The prisoner spoke her final words. The executioner put a noose around her neck. He tightened it. Then he pushed her off the ladder. All the while, the crowd continued its cruel mockery.

Death by hanging was a terrible sight. Usually the prisoner's neck did not break, so death was not quick. Instead, the prisoner swung side to side, slowly choking to death. Sometimes death took several minutes. Sometimes it took much longer.

The executioner put a hood over each prisoner's head before pushing her off the ladder. This hood was meant to keep the crowd from seeing the person's face in the agony of death.

One by one, the five convicted witches were hanged. As each prisoner stood on the ladder, she again said that she was innocent. Each of the prisoners prayed to God. Some also prayed that God would forgive those who falsely accused them.

Rebecca Nurse went to her death with quiet dignity. Sarah Wilds, Elizabeth How, and Susannah Martin had also resigned themselves to dying. But Sarah Good, always known for her temper, showed it to the very end.

As Sarah approached the ladder, Reverend Nicholas Noyes spoke to her. He urged her to confess her guilt.

"You are a witch," he said. "You know it is true. Confess now."

Sarah turned to the minister angrily.

"You are a liar!" she snarled. "I am no more a witch than you are a wizard. And I say this to you. If you take my life, God will give you blood to drink!"

A minute later, Sarah Good was hanged.

It is said that Sarah's last words to the minister were remembered many years later. As Nicholas Noyes lay on his death bed, he began to cough. Blood flowed from the minister's mouth. Then he died.

After the hangings, the five women were cut down. Their bodies were handled with no more respect than Bridget Bishop's body had received. They were buried, without prayer, in the rocks along the hillside. There they remained—except for one.

Under cover of night, several members of Rebecca Nurse's family returned to Gallows Hill. They found Rebecca's body and took it down the hill.

They buried Rebecca in an unmarked grave. The exact location of that grave remains a secret to this day.

Chapter 33

The next witchcraft trials began on August 5. Six accused witches faced the court, four men and two women. They were: George Burroughs, John and Elizabeth Proctor, George Jacobs, John Willard, and Martha Carrier. These six stood no better chance than any of the witches already hanged.

The trial that drew the most attention was that of George Burroughs. The minister was accused of more than just acts of witchcraft, though these alone would have been enough to hang him. Burroughs had been named—first by Deliverance Hobbs, then by Abigail Williams and Mary Warren—as the leader of the witches. It was he who had told other witches to bewitch the people of Salem Village.

Burroughs had faced two of the judges before. William Stoughton and Samuel Sewall had been present at his hearing in May. It was Stoughton who had ordered him to jail.

The evidence against Burroughs mounted quickly. For the minister, the trial was a nightmare relived. Again the afflicted girls had their wild fits. Again witness after witness testified against him. They spoke of his supernatural strength, of his evil deeds. They told how the ghosts of his dead wives accused him of murder. Many recently confessed witches added new testimony. Several said they saw the minister leading witch services.

There was never any doubt what the verdict would be. George Burroughs was found guilty. So were John and Elizabeth Proctor, George Jacobs, John Willard, and Martha Carrier. All but one were sentenced to hang on August 19.

Only Elizabeth Proctor was spared, at least for the present. Elizabeth was pregnant. Her baby would be the child of a witch and a wizard. But even so, the judges would not put an innocent, unborn child to death.

Chapter 34

One of the six prisoners brought to trial on August 5 was Martha Carrier. Martha had been the first accused witch from the town of Andover. But she was far from the last. In fact, more people from Andover were arrested than from any other place, including Salem Village.

Much of the witchcraft hysteria in Andover can be traced to Salem Village. A man named Joseph Ballard was a constable in Andover. (He was the constable who brought Martha Carrier to Salem for trial.) When Ballard's wife became ill, he feared that witchcraft might be the cause.

Ballard had heard that Salem's afflicted girls could see witches. So he sent for them. Ann Putnam, Mary Walcott, and several other girls were pleased to go. The invitation to Andover made them feel more special than ever.

Andover lies northwest of Salem Village. Ann, Mary, and the other girls traveled there by horse. Upon their arrival, they were treated like celebrities. Ballard's friends and neighbors rushed to greet them. They spoke to the girls with great respect. So did many other citizens of the town. Everyone had heard the frightening stories about Salem's witches. If these girls could spot any witches in Andover, they were surely welcome.

The afflicted girls did not disappoint them. They identified one witch after another, mostly by means of the touch test. An Andover official named Dudley Bradstreet began writing out arrest warrants. (Bradstreet was the son of the Massachusetts colony's former governor, Simon Bradstreet.) As fast as he would write the warrant for one witch, the girls would point out another.

Bradstreet wrote out ten warrants. Then he wrote another ten. And another. Finally, after he had written forty warrants, Bradstreet stopped. Enough was enough. No one had expected so many witches in such a small town. At this rate, the girls would name half the citizens of Andover! And nearly all their accusations were based on the touch test alone.

Bradstreet said that he would write no more arrest warrants. Soon after his refusal, Bradstreet himself was named a witch. He knew the charge was false, but he wasn't taking any chances. He and his wife fled from Andover.

As the girls found more and more witches, a

near panic broke out in the town. Some of Andover's people began having fits like those of the afflicted girls. Some claimed that they, too, could see specters. Andover's afflicted citizens began adding their own accusations to those made by Salem's girls. Everyone was swept up in talk of witches and the Devil. People even put a *dog* to death on suspicion of witchcraft.

Ann Putnam, Mary Walcott, and the others were so convincing that some of the accused witches confessed. In their fear, they believed that if the afflicted girls said they were witches, then it must be true.

In Andover, as in Salem Village, one confession often led to another. And as more people confessed, the fires of witchcraft burned ever brighter. More accusations led to even more confessions, adding fuel to the flames. Before the witch hunt was over, more than fifty people in Salem Village, Andover, and other towns had confessed to witchcraft!

Some confessions contained startling details. For example, William Barker of Andover said he had been "in the Devil's snare" for three years. He explained that the Devil planned to abolish all churches. The Devil also intended to attack the whole country, starting with Salem. More than three hundred witches were helping the Devil carry out his evil plans, Barker said.

Barker's confession increased people's worries. They saw that they were under attack by a large number of witches working together. Other accused witches made similar confessions. Some talked about meetings of witches like those Deliverance Hobbs had described. Often, they named some of the witches at the meetings. At times, people reported seeing witches who had already been hanged.

Interestingly, Andover's witch hunt ended almost as quickly as it began. A respected gentleman in Boston learned that accusers in Andover had called him a witch. He was furious. Who dared to dirty his good name? he wanted to know.

Then this gentleman did something no one else had thought to do. He took legal action. He demanded one thousand pounds from his accusers for their false charges.

In 1692, one thousand pounds was a huge amount of money. Apparently, it was so huge that it silenced the accusers. No further charges against the Boston gentleman were made. Before long, all other accusations in Andover stopped too.

Chapter 35

On August 19, five more prisoners rode the cart up Gallows Hill. This time four were men: George Burroughs, John Proctor, John Willard, and George Jacobs. The only woman among them was Martha Carrier of Andover.

The noisy crowd that walked with the cart was bigger than ever. Many had come to see George Burroughs hang. He was, after all, the leader of the witches. The event had drawn such important people as Judge Samuel Sewall, Reverend John Hale of Beverly, and Reverend Nicholas Noyes of Salem Town. Even the well-known minister Cotton Mather had come from Boston.

Once more, the cart stopped near the top of the hill. The convicted witches looked up at the tall oak tree. They saw the ladder propped against the branch, the dangling nooses.

The executioner waited. George Burroughs was brought forward. The large crowd grew noisier. Some were laughing.

As Burroughs stood on the ladder, he was allowed to say his last words. He gazed around at the crowd. Then he began to speak. The people's voices died down.

Burroughs' speech was solemn and moving. His elegant words stopped all the shouts and laughter. The people listened, their faces somber. Burroughs declared his innocence and prayed to God. He asked God to forgive false witnesses. His words and the emotion behind them touched the crowd. Some spectators began to weep.

Burroughs ended by reciting the Lord's Prayer. As soon as he began, a murmur rippled through the crowd. Witches sometimes said the Lord's Prayer backwards at their meetings, but not forwards. Everyone knew it was impossible for a witch to say the Lord's Prayer correctly.

Yet, Burroughs did say it. And he said it perfectly.

When he had finished, some spectators wondered aloud whether George Burroughs could truly be guilty. He appeared so composed. He had spoken so sincerely. And he had said the Lord's Prayer without so much as a pause.

One of the afflicted girls shouted that she had seen a dark shape standing beside Burroughs. This shape had told him what to say. Other afflicted girls quickly agreed.

But the crowd paid little attention. Burroughs' words still rang in their ears. Could a true wizard have spoken so convincingly?

Some people began to move forward. For a moment, it seemed that they would try to stop the hanging.

Suddenly, Cotton Mather climbed onto his horse. He addressed the crowd. He reminded them of what Reverend Deodat Lawson had once said: "Satan never works more like the Prince of Darkness than when he looks most like an angel of light." Don't be fooled! Mather urged the people. Burroughs is not the innocent person he claims to be. He is guilty of witchcraft!

Mather succeeded in quieting the crowd. There were still some who had doubts. But no one tried to stop the execution. George Burroughs was hanged.

John Proctor, John Willard, George Jacobs, and Martha Carrier were also hanged. But like Burroughs—perhaps inspired by him—they too died with great dignity. They too prayed to God and asked for forgiveness for those who wrongly condemned them. They prayed that theirs would be the last innocent lives taken.

The crowd was unusually silent as these prisoners were hanged. Afterwards, most spectators remained quiet as the five bodies were added to those already buried on the rocky hillside.

Eleven prisoners had now been executed for witchcraft. More hangings would follow. But

August 19 would not soon be forgotten. Never before had so many people publicly shown sympathy for convicted witches. Never before had so many publicly shown doubt.

Still, the prisons were full, and the hearings and trials were continuing. The judges were still accepting spectral evidence. More prisoners would die before the witch-hunt madness ended.

Chapter 36

On September 9, the Court of Oyer and Terminer found six more prisoners guilty. All were sentenced to hang. Among the six were Mary Easty, one of Rebecca Nurse's sisters, and Martha Corey. Martha had been the fourth person accused and arrested in Salem Village. Her hearing had occurred almost six months earlier. Since then, she had been in prison awaiting trial.

On September 17, another set of trials took place. The court sentenced nine more prisoners to death. That another fifteen accused witches had been condemned in just over a week was shocking. But two days later, another event took place that was perhaps even more shocking.

In addition to Martha Corey, Giles Corey too was brought before the court in September. Giles was Martha's eighty-year-old husband. Giles had earned a reputation as a cross and stubborn man. But he was also a man who stood up against those who tried to wrong him.

Giles knew that if the court found him guilty, his property would be seized by the sheriff. Giles was determined not to let this happen. He wanted his property to pass on to his relatives.

Before prisoners could be tried, they had to enter a plea. That is, they had to say whether they were innocent or guilty. Giles decided to keep silent. If he did not enter a plea, he could not be put on trial.

In court, the judges asked Giles to make his plea. He refused. If I'm tried, Giles told them, the same people who spoke against me at the hearing will speak against me again. What chance will I have? Every accused person who's faced this court and the afflicted girls has been found guilty. So kill me if you will, Giles said. But I won't enter a plea.

Giles was probably correct about his chances. But the judges were not pleased. They reminded him that under the law, he could be forced—by torture—to enter a plea.

Still Giles refused. For him, this was now more than just a matter of keeping his property. Giles was making a protest against the court itself, the court that had convicted his wife.

Constables took Giles to a field. They made him lie on his back. Then they placed a wide wooden board on top of him. They asked him again if he would enter a plea. Giles kept silent.

The constables put a heavy rock on top of the board. Then another. And another. Once more they asked Giles to make a plea. Giles said nothing.

Hours passed. The constables added more rocks, one by one. The load pressing on Giles' chest grew heavier and heavier. Breathing became harder and harder for him.

Again Giles was asked to enter a plea. His face red, Giles managed to gasp only two words:

"More weight."

After nearly two days, the awful spectacle finally ended. Giles Corey was dead.

The death of Giles Corey made many people uneasy. Giles was not a popular man. But who could not be impressed by his stubborn courage? More than one witness wondered if a guilty man would have chosen such a terrible death.

What Giles' wife Martha thought when she heard how her husband died is not known. Certainly, Martha Corey had other worries on her mind. She herself was scheduled to hang in just three days.

Chapter 37

On September 22, another cart of prisoners traveled the road to Gallows Hill. Seven women and one man were packed into this cart, three more prisoners than ever before. The condemned came from various towns: Salem, Andover, Topsfield, and Marblehead.

Of the fifteen prisoners tried and convicted in September, nearly half had managed to avoid the noose. The court spared five because they confessed. The judges still looked with favor on those who confessed and testified against others. Another prisoner was spared because she was pregnant. As in the case of Elizabeth Proctor, the judges would not condemn to death an unborn child. And one prisoner, a well-to-do older woman from Salisbury named Mary Bradbury, had escaped from prison with the aid of her friends.

The convicted witches who had not been

spared included Martha Corey and Mary Easty, Rebecca Nurse's sister. The one man aboard the cart bound for Gallows Hill was Samuel Wardwell of Andover. Besides his own fate, Wardwell had other concerns. His wife had also been arrested for witchcraft. She had not yet been tried. But with her in prison too, there was no one to care for their young children.

As always, a crowd accompanied the creaking cart as it climbed the steep hill. At one point, a wheel got stuck, and the cart could not move. The afflicted girls immediately cried out that the Devil was holding back the cart. It seemed as if the girls could explain the evil behind any event.

None of the eight people on the cart held any hope of escaping the noose. They knew that eleven prisoners had been hanged before them, and one man had been tortured to death. The crowd showed no signs of sympathy. Whatever regrets spectators may have felt at the August 19 hangings seemed to have faded. People shouted at the prisoners, taunted them, called them witches and worse.

Mary Easty had already given up all hope several days earlier. Knowing she was going to die, Mary tried to help others. She sent an emotional letter to the judges and ministers. In her letter, Mary explained that she knew the legal process was flawed because she was innocent. "I know not the least thing of witchcraft," she wrote. Mary pleaded not to save her own life but to keep other innocent people from being wrongfully executed. She urged the judges not to trust the false testimony of afflicted girls and confessing witches. They have lied about me, she said, and they are lying about others.

Mary's letter drew no response from the judges. However, as Mary stood on the ladder on Gallows Hill, her heartfelt last words did draw a response from the people. She prayed to God and insisted once more that she was innocent. Then she tenderly said goodbye to her husband, her children, and her friends. When she was finished, many spectators wiped tears from their eyes.

Even so, Mary Easty was hanged. So were Martha Corey and Samuel Wardwell. And so were the five other convicted witches who had climbed Gallows Hill on September 22.

After all eight had been executed, Reverend Nicholas Noyes looked at the swinging bodies.

"What a sad thing to see eight firebrands of hell hanging there," he commented.

Some in the crowd agreed. Some even wondered whether all those hanged had truly been "firebrands of hell." Everyone feared and hated witches. But it was hard not to feel sorry for people like Mary Easty. It was hard to feel no pity as the condemned said prayers and bid their last goodbyes to loved ones. It was hard to believe that so many people were agents of the Devil.

Chapter 38

As the summer of 1692 ended, the mood in Salem and nearby towns was changing. Recent events had left a growing number of people troubled. For many, fear was slowly giving way to doubt.

Several things helped cause the shift in mood. Four months had passed since Governor Phips set up the Court of Oyer and Terminer. Everyone had hoped the court would bring a quick end to the witchcraft scare. But this had not happened. Rather, to some people it seemed that the court had made matters worse.

Prisons were more crowded than ever. One hundred and fifty men, women, and even children were now in jail. Some two hundred more people had been accused. And despite all the imprisonments and executions, the situation had not improved. The afflicted girls were still having fits. More people were claiming to be afflicted. And more prisoners were confessing and accusing others.

The deaths of twenty people, too, had contributed to the change in mood. In particular, the hangings of Rebecca Nurse, George Burroughs, Mary Easty, and John Proctor had raised doubts in people's minds. So had the cruel death of Giles Corey.

The most troubling issue continued to be the matter of spectral evidence. From the start, some people had questioned whether such evidence could be trusted. Most Massachusetts ministers had expressed doubt.

In early October, Increase Mather, the father of Cotton Mather, gave voice to what many people were thinking. Increase was a leading Boston minister and an important man in Massachusetts. It had been he who brought the colony's new charter from England in May.

Mather gave a sermon to a group of ministers. The sermon was later published as an essay. It was called *Cases of Conscience Concerning Evil Spirits Personating Men.* Fourteen other ministers signed the work to show their agreement. People all over Massachusetts read and discussed *Cases of Conscience.* In his essay, Mather strongly challenged the methods of the Court of Oyer and Terminer. He cast great doubt on the use of spectral evidence to convict witches. He warned against believing the testimony of confessing witches. He also spoke out strongly against the touch test.

Mather stressed that anyone may be falsely accused of witchcraft. For this reason, convictions should be based only on absolute proof of guilt.

"Better that ten suspected witches should escape than one innocent person should be condemned," Mather wrote.

Just days after Mather's sermon, another respected person spoke out. He was Thomas Brattle, a Boston scientist and merchant. Brattle circulated a sharply worded letter. The letter condemned the methods of the witch hunt.

Brattle criticized the judges for believing the afflicted girls. He denounced the confessions made by accused witches. He attacked the use of spectral evidence. He argued against witch's marks and the touch test.

While Mather and Brattle were protesting, the afflicted girls were still naming witches. In fact, their reckless accusations added to people's doubts. The afflicted girls were finally going too far.

They made charges of witchcraft against respected ministers and rich merchants. They accused the mother-in-law of magistrate Jonathan Corwin and accused the sons of former governor Simon Bradstreet. They even accused Governor Phips' wife!

By mid-October, reason at last won out over fear. Governor Phips ordered that no more people be put in prison on charges of witchcraft. Trials were postponed. The fate of all the people already in jail was still to be decided.

On October 29, the governor dismissed the Court of Oyer and Terminer. There would be no more witches hanged in Salem.

Chapter 39

The afflicted girls gradually lost their hold on the people. By November, their power and influence had all but faded away. People no longer believed in them.

One afternoon, several of the girls were walking across a bridge. They passed an old woman. The girls stared at her. Then they began having fits. "Witch!" they all cried.

A few months before, such an event would have drawn a crowd. No doubt the accused witch would have been arrested. But on this cold fall day, people nearby paid little attention. They looked at the girls. They glanced at the woman. And then they went on about their business. The afflicted girls had no choice but to get back on their feet and continue on their way.

As people in Salem and other towns stopped taking them seriously, the girls ceased making accusations.

Chapter 40

While the government discussed what to do next, one hundred and fifty accused witches waited in jail. These prisoners now felt some hope. Yet, the days and weeks passed slowly. The prisoners feared they might remain in jail for a long time to come.

Now and then, other people were accused of witchcraft. But no one else went to prison. Instead, persons newly accused were allowed bail. That is, they left a sum of money with the court to guarantee that they would appear for trial. In return, they were temporarily set free.

The governor even let out on bail some prisoners already in jail. Many children were released. So were prisoners unlikely to survive the cold weather in unheated cells. A few prisoners whose absence caused their families great hardship were also granted bail.

As winter set in, temperatures fell. The many

prisoners not lucky enough to be out on bail huddled in their dark and dirty cells. They waited.

Finally, starting in January, 1693, a new Superior Court began trying the accused witches. Once again, William Stoughton was made chief judge. Four other judges joined him at the court's first session. Three had also served on the Court of Oyer and Terminer. The fourth was Thomas Danforth. Danforth was the former deputy governor who had run the Salem Town hearings in April.

That the same people who had served before were serving again was not as odd as it might seem. True, the court's methods had been questioned. However, the judges themselves were still highly respected.

Besides, there were two key differences between the new Superior Court and the Court of Oyer and Terminer. First, the judges and jury would no longer consider spectral evidence. Governor Phips had ordered this on the advice of the clergy.

Second, the new Massachusetts charter changed the rules about who could serve on a jury. No longer could only church members be jurors, as had been the case. Now non-church members could also serve. This was important. Non-church members were not as quick to believe someone was a witch.

Between January and May, the Superior Court tried more than fifty accused witches. These trials turned out very differently from the earlier ones. Only three people were found guilty. All three had confessed.

In the past, prisoners who confessed were spared. It was those who claimed innocence who were sentenced to death. But times had changed. Confessing witches were no longer needed to name other witches. Judge Stoughton ordered Sarah Wardwell and the other two convicted witches to hang.

Governor Phips, however, had other plans. He ordered all three released. He also released five other prisoners condemned by the Court of Oyer and Terminer. One was Elizabeth Proctor. She left jail holding her new baby. This was the child who had saved the pregnant Elizabeth from hanging.

Stoughton was in court when he heard what the governor had done. He was furious. He stormed out. Despite all that had happened, Stoughton remained firm in his views. He could not understand why Phips would stand in the way of justice.

By May of 1693, Governor Phips had had enough of witch trials. He ordered a general pardon of all accused witches still in prison. More than one hundred prisoners were set free.

Among them was Sarah Cloyce, sister of Rebecca Nurse and Mary Easty.

Despite the pardon, not every released prisoner could leave. Prisoners had to pay for their imprisonment. Cost included room and board, clothes, court fees, and various other expenses. The longer a prisoner was in jail, the higher the costs. Some prisoners did not have enough money to pay the money due. They could not get out of jail unless relatives or friends paid their bill. More than one prisoner died in jail.

One prisoner who could not afford to pay was Tituba. Her confession more than a year ago had played a key part in fueling the witch hunt. She had been in prison ever since.

Reverend Parris refused to pay Tituba's bill. However, he sold the slave for an amount equal to what she owed. Who bought Tituba and what became of her after her release is not known. Also unknown is what happened to her husband, John Indian. John had testified against Sarah Cloyce, Elizabeth Proctor, and others. He may well have been sold along with Tituba.

Prisoners faced more hardship after their release from jail. Many families had lost one or more members. Children were often in a sorry state. Some had managed to survive only by begging for food.

Many prisoners found that officials had taken away their property. Others had to sell their farms to pay prison costs and rising taxes. Some had so little money left that they lived in poverty.

Numerous farms had been neglected for months. Many farmers had been in prison. Many more had lost time traveling to see jailed relatives and attend hearings and trials. Fields had not been plowed. Crops had not been harvested. Animals had not been tended. Farmhouses, barns, fences, and roads had not been maintained.

Fewer crops led to food shortages. Suffering was widespread. The witchcraft scare was over, but its impact on the people would be felt for a long time to come.

Chapter 41

As Salem Village struggled to recover, people muttered about Reverend Samuel Parris. Before the witch hunt, the minister had had many enemies. Now he had more.

Some people blamed Reverend Parris for starting and encouraging the witch hunt. Some said he had always worried more about his own welfare than anyone else's. Many now criticized the minister for his actions.

People said he had been too quick to believe the worst about good church members like Rebecca Nurse. Why had the minister not been more charitable? Why had he been so ready to accept the afflicted girls' charges? Why had he promoted "the Devil's accusations"? Why had he been so willing to condemn? And with all that had happened, why did the minister still stubbornly refuse to admit the possibility that he might have been wrong?

Tituba, too, added her voice to those that spoke against Reverend Parris. She accused the minister of having forced her to confess to witchcraft.

Some villagers stopped coming to Reverend Parris' church services. He was not even fit to be minister, they said. Withhold his salary! some demanded.

For nearly two years, Reverend Parris tried to defend himself against those who criticized him. He argued with them. He accused them of treating him unfairly.

Finally, in the fall of 1694, Reverend Parris changed his tone. He made an emotional speech. He apologized and admitted that perhaps he had been wrong. Maybe he should not have taken spectral evidence as seriously as he did. Maybe he should have allowed for the possibility that the Devil could take the shape of innocent people. Maybe he should not have given so much weight to the words of the afflicted girls.

Reverend Parris asked for forgiveness for his mistakes. But the minister's speech came too late. Too many people in the village opposed him.

Reverend Parris managed to cling to his position until 1697. Then the minister gave up. He left Salem Village.

Chapter 42

Reverend Parris was not the only person to voice regrets. The same year the minister left Salem Village, twelve jurors signed a public letter of apology. In the letter, the jurors said that they now realized their errors. They only wished they could undo them. The jurors expressed deep sorrow for having brought upon themselves and others "the guilt of innocent blood." They asked for forgiveness from God and from the people.

Similar feelings were expressed by Judge Samuel Sewall. He asked for God's pardon for his "blame and shame" in the Court of Oyer and Terminer. Each year for the rest of his life, Sewall set aside a personal day for fasting and repenting.

Sewall, however, was unusual. Most officials involved in the witch hunt saw no reason to make apologies. They had done what they thought was right and necessary. For example, neither John Hathorne nor William Stoughton changed his views. Both men continued to have successful careers.

As for the afflicted girls, little is known of what happened to them. Betty Parris gradually recovered after her parents sent her away from Salem Village. Later, she got married.

Many of the other afflicted girls also got married, including Mercy Lewis, Mary Walcott, and Elizabeth Booth. What became of Abigail Williams and Elizabeth Hubbard is unknown. Some said that Abigail never fully recovered. Others said that she led a troubled life.

Ann Putnam did not marry. While a number of the other girls left Salem Village, Ann did not. Both of her parents died in 1699, when she was nineteen. She then cared for her nine sisters and brothers.

Ann was still living in Salem Village in 1706. That year, she made a remarkable public statement. The minister read her words aloud to the crowded meetinghouse. Twenty-six-year-old Ann Putnam stood, head bowed, as the minister read.

In the statement, Ann expressed regret for her part in accusing innocent people. She said that "a great delusion of Satan" had deceived her. She had not meant to harm anyone. "I did it not out of any anger, malice, or ill will." The Devil had made her act as she did.

Ann said that she was especially sorry for having accused Rebecca Nurse and her two sisters. She begged forgiveness from God and from all those to whom she had caused sorrow.

The young woman's words seemed sincere. But the full truth behind what Ann Putnam said and did when she was only twelve is impossible to know.

Ann lived for eleven more years. Her health was often poor. She died in 1716, when she was thirty-seven.

Chapter 43

After the witchcraft trials, the people of Salem and other towns got on with their lives. But the freed prisoners and the relatives of the hanged prisoners were troubled. Although Governor Phips had pardoned the accused witches, charges of witchcraft left a stain on their reputations. The survivors wanted the government to clear the names of those accused. They also wanted repayment for their financial losses.

In 1703, the Massachusetts government banned spectral evidence. The government also made a statement against past convictions based on such evidence.

Victims of the witch hunt were not satisfied. The government's action was far too weak in view of what the victims had suffered.

Finally, in 1710, the government formally cleared the names of some—but not all—accused witches. Those people for whom relatives or friends had specifically pleaded were cleared. Those with no one to speak for them, such as Bridget Bishop, were not.

In 1711, the government agreed to pay various sums of money to the relatives of twenty-four prisoners. These were prisoners who had been hanged, had died in jail, or had been imprisoned for many months.

Not until 1957, more than two hundred years later, did Massachusetts officially clear the names of all other accused witches.

Today, a memorial dedicated to victims of "the Salem Village Witchcraft Hysteria" stands in Danvers, Massachusetts.

Afterword

The events in Salem Village raised many questions. Historians are still trying to answer some of those questions today.

If not witchcraft, then what did cause the afflicted girls to have fits? Were the girls merely pretending? Did the afflicted girls truly believe the charges they made?

There are many theories about the behavior of Abigail Williams, Ann Putnam, and the other girls. Certainly, fear played a big part in what happened. Like most others of their time, the girls feared the Devil. They also feared witches, who were the Devil's agents.

When the egg white in the glass—"a tool of the Devil"—revealed a coffin, Betty Parris and her cousin Abigail were doubly afraid. The girls knew they would be severely punished if their games were discovered. But much more frightening was the possibility that they had indeed done "Devil's work."

The intense fear and stress that the girls felt probably led to hysteria. Hysteria is a mental or emotional disorder that can have various symptoms. Some of these symptoms can be physical. Hysterical people may have fits. They may complain of pains. They may choke, scream, cry, or babble. They may see things that aren't there.

Hysteria could explain the violent fits of the afflicted girls. It could also explain why the girls saw, or thought they saw, specters.

Hysteria is also, in a way, "catching." Under certain conditions, its symptoms can spread from one person to another. When hysteria spreads to a large number of people, it's often called "mass hysteria."

The hysteria that began with Betty and Abigail may have rapidly spread to Ann Putnam, Elizabeth Hubbard, and the other girls. The girls were friends. Many of them had listened to Tituba's stories about magic and fortune-telling. A number of them had taken part in the forbidden games. All of them shared Betty and Abigail's fears about Satan and witches. All of them felt the emotional stress of Puritan strictness.

The afflicted girls' hysteria could also have affected others in Salem Village. Talk of witchcraft added to the villagers' fears. As these fears increased, the hysteria spread. People were looking for witches and specters. They believed in them. They *expected* to see them. So, witches and specters were what many of the people did see.

Still, hysteria may not have been the only factor at work. What if Doctor Griggs had never said the girls were bewitched? What if the girls had not been pressured to name witches? Maybe they would never have set a witch hunt in motion.

Maybe once the girls were swept up by the witchcraft wave they saw no way out. One event rapidly led to another. Things went out of control. Before long, they became celebrities. Everyone paid attention to them. Never before had the girls had so much power over others. It was a thrilling feeling. When people started getting arrested and the hearings began, it was too late for the girls to do anything but go along.

Divisions within Salem may also have contributed to the witch hunt. There was a long history of conflict between different groups of people. For example, farmers and merchants had clashed over several matters. Groups had also quarreled over the choice of ministers. Thomas Putnam and his family supported Reverend Samuel Parris. Others in Salem opposed both Parris and the Putnams.

Did the Putnams use the witchcraft scare to attack their enemies? Some insist they did. Thomas Putnam signed more formal complaints against people for witchcraft than any other person. His daughter, wife, and servant were among the afflicted. Did Thomas Putnam influence these people? Did he put words in any of their mouths?

There is probably no one answer to the question of how it all happened. Like a puzzle, many pieces came together to form the whole.

Still, historians continue to propose theories about the events in Salem. One theory has to do with a fungus called ergot. Grain infected by this fungus can cause hallucinations if eaten. Was the rye flour in Salem in 1692 infected by this fungus? If so, the visions that the afflicted girls and others saw may have been ergot hallucinations.

Similarly, it's been suggested that some visions may have resulted from herbs. Plant parts were often brewed in hot water to make medicine. Such herbal medicines could cause hallucinations or other symptoms if made or used incorrectly.

Such theories about chemically caused visions are interesting. However, they are not widely accepted. They leave too many unanswered questions.

The whole truth about the Salem witch hunt may never be known. However, historians will continue to study the events of 1692. What they learn may teach us not only about history but also about human nature.